a love story in a utopian future

Janette Rainwater

*For Karen Workcuff
with much love.
Janette Rainwater
11 January 2008*

iUniverse, Inc.

New York Lincoln Shanghai

2060

a love story in a utopian future

iUniverse books may be ordered through booksellers or by contacting:

iUniverse
2021 Pine Lake Road, Suite 100
Lincoln, NE 68512
www.iuniverse.com
1-800-Authors (1-800-288-4677)

Because of the dynamic nature of the Internet, any Web addresses or links contained in this book may have changed since publication and may no longer be valid.

This is a work of fiction. All of the characters, names, incidents, organizations, and dialogue in this novel are either the products of the author's imagination or are used fictitiously.

ISBN: 978-0-595-42379-8 (pbk)
ISBN: 978-0-595-86715-8 (ebk)

Printed in the United States of America

2060

Also by Janette Rainwater

You're in Charge: A Guide to Becoming Your Own Therapist

Vision: How, Why, and What We See

A Dragon in a Wagon

The Return: A Book for Frances about Life and Death

МОСКВА—ЛОС-АНДЖЕЛЕС

(Moscow—Los Angeles, or How to Learn the English Language)

Preface

This is not a story that I consciously started out to write. In the summer of 2006, I would awaken most mornings after having dreamed of a scene from a year that appeared to be 2060. For many years, I have faithfully written down all vivid dreams; as a psychologist, I have encouraged clients and patients to do the same thing as part of their therapy.

Initially, I considered these dreams and the time taken to record them as a distraction from my main, long-term writing project—an annotated chronology of the major events of the twentieth century, told from a progressive perspective. Its title is *From the New Deal to the Raw Deal.* (For excerpts, see www.janrainwater.com.)

Other than changing the story to the past tense—the action in the dreams felt very present-tense, as in a movie—and checking the facts about Cumbre Vieja, a volcano that plays a major role in this novel, there was no Jan-the-writer writing the first parts of *2060.* Katie's lecture is almost verbatim as I heard it in my dreams. I have been asked if this was something that was "channeled." No, it was my unconscious mind speaking—the part of me that was, and is, so very upset about the direction this country has taken regarding Iraq, global warming, and so on.

I want to thank the many friends who have read this and urged me to publish it (after continuing to develop the characters.) The list is too long to include here, but you know who you are, and I am most grateful. Special thanks to Simona Gayauskas for the author photo.

Let's dedicate *2060* to all who have dreams and visions of a more equitable and compassionate society.

Auditorium, Roberts Hall, Tuesday, 2:30 PM

Katie Kendall had already started her lecture when Angela slipped into the crowded auditorium and found a seat near the back.

"When the men first started dying, some people immediately thought that 'the terrorists' had released a virus to eradicate our menfolk ..."

Oh, dear, thought Angela, *she's finished talking about her childhood and the Old Days, and that's the part I really wanted to hear.* She fidgeted with her flyer:

Katie Kendall

Professor Emeritus of Genetics
Former Council Board Member

On Her 80th Birthday
Talks about
Her Past
The Present
Our Future

Auditorium, Roberts Hall
Tuesday, August 17, 2060 at 2 PM

Katie continued: "President Bush, the second one, had used 'terrorism' as a tool to induce fear and maintain control—much like administrations after World War II had used the fear of communism ..."

Katie paused to assess the impact of her words on her audience, and laughed. "No, I wasn't around for the major years of the Cold War; I'm really not *that* old. But I heard so much about it from my grandmother that I might as well have lived through it myself.

"Some of the famous men who died in the early stages of the Gender-Specific Virus were men in the Bush administration of the old United States. Possibly one of the very first was the vice president, who disappeared from view in the spring of 2008. At first, most of us had assumed that he was just in his famous 'undisclosed location.' Many people in the peace movement secretly applauded when the former Secretary of Defense succumbed. Most people openly cheered when a massive sea-air evacuation of the troops and American civilian personnel was ordered from that very unpopular war in Iraq.

"Initially, the GSV seemed to attack only men over the age of fifty. This assumption led to another early erroneous hypothesis—that taking Viagra or another of the drugs that enhanced erectile function had made these men vulnerable. That rumor probably got started because one of the first famous victims was an ex-senator who had made TV commercials for one of these drugs. But that was not true; there was no correlation. By the 2008 election, there weren't many men over fifty left alive, or at least visible. Some of them had simply dropped dead without warning; some died a few days after developing a very high fever; many went into hiding, fearing that they could catch the virus from another man. And some committed suicide. By the time of the Great Disaster in 2010, most mothers of young boys were keeping them out of school and not allowing them out of the house. Most of the young men had gone into hiding. I don't have the figures on the mortality rates with me—let's just say that the undertakers were not underemployed."

Angela was enjoying watching this woman whom she admired so much—not just her great teaching ability, but her obvious common sense and humanity as well. Her voice was so strong, her back so straight. The only indications of her age were the cane hanging from the edge of the lectern and her long, snow-white hair, which she had today coiled into a bun at the nape of her neck instead of wearing it in the usual ponytail down her back. Angela unconsciously twisted her own black ponytail into a similar bun and then let it fall free.

Katie was enjoying her story. "I'm sure you have all heard that President Bush resigned before his term was up and went into hiding at his ranch in Texas. One by one, his male cabinet members and senior members of Congress either died or also went into isolation. The Speaker of the House became, by default, the acting president, and she easily won election in 2008. She and the surgeon general, also a woman, were two of the real heroines of this century. Between them, they made some crucial decisions that prepared us for the Great Disaster and the survival of at least a portion of our society."

Angela surveyed the auditorium. It was one of the larger university lecture halls, and it had been festooned with crepe banners and signs reading "80" and "Kudos to Katie." She recognized many of the women present, mostly a mix of historians and biologists.

"We biologists knew that this Mysterious Virus, as it was first called by the public, was not exclusive to the United States, but was happening all over the world. Here in California and elsewhere on the West Coast, it was called the Mysterious *East Coast* Virus, as the sudden mortality of men over fifty was first noticed there. I was returning from a trip to remote areas of Latin America when the Great Disaster struck. In the remote native villages that we visited, the men had been dying off even more rapidly than in the United States and Europe. In those communities, the women had not been educated and did not have the skills to take over from the men. We know now that those places later became practically Stone-Age communities. If there are any people left there today, they would probably be just a few old women. No sperm banks there!

"Possibly the most important decision—one that was unknown to the general public at the time—was the deputizing of women biologists to take charge of the many sperm banks in the United States. They transferred all the sperm donations to specially constructed buildings that had their own generators and supplies of fuel. I was part of the team of geneticists that commandeered the sperm banks in New England. And, up until the Great Disaster, I was a member of the Genetics Committee in Boston. It was we who made those difficult decisions about which women would receive sperm and whose sperm they would get."

At this point, Katie was distracted by a woman who was standing and waving her white card in the air. "If your question pertains to something I've just said," Katie said to her, "please hand it to one of the assistants. Otherwise, hand in your cards at the break, and I will try to answer all of them before we end today."

There was an enthusiastic waving of hands above heads in agreement, applauding Katie's instructions to the woman, and Katie continued: "Those sperm bank locations are secret. Even if I knew where our local ones were, I wouldn't tell you. Here in Greater Los Angeles—and elsewhere on the West Coast—we have enough sperm to last until the end of the century. And we have hopes that, long before that time, we will have conquered the virus, and the young men and boys will be able to come out into the world. Perhaps you've heard that there are already a few young men who are venturing out of their homes?"

There was a murmur of voices in the audience: "So the rumor is true!" "My brother Ben is fifteen and has major cabin fever." "We have a fifteen-year-old in our commune, too; he's threatening to run away."

Katie smiled and waited until the voices had hushed. "I know that many of you are here today," she continued, "not to celebrate the birthday of an eighty-year-old woman, but in hopes of getting preferential treatment as a sperm recipient. Be sure to say so on your card, and you will be contacted. I am not a member of the section of the Genetics Committee that evaluates recipients for insemination, but I will see that your requests go to the right place.

"Please understand that if you are not accepted, there is nothing wrong with you *per se*. Supplies are limited, and demand is great, so we must make the survival of our society the highest priority. We take into consideration the age and health of the applying woman, the health history of her parents and grandparents, and also the health history of her sperm-donor father. We might also look at the health history of a sperm-donor grandfather. How many of you here have a sperm-donor grandfather?"

Angela raised her hand and looked around to see how many other hands had been raised. In an auditorium packed with more than a thousand women of varying ages, it appeared that about two-thirds of them could trace their sperm-donor lineage back two generations.

"Quite a number!" Katie said. "Thank goodness that those records have been kept! We will also need to know whether your request is from a partnership and, if so, whether one of the women will be willing to stay home and homeschool the child if it turns out to be a boy. All recipients must make a commitment to stay in touch with the Genetics Committee, as we need to monitor the health and progress of the new children."

Angela tuned out the lecture at this point and debated with herself, *Of course, Cameron wants me to submit my name. She certainly made it clear this morning ... tried to make me promise that I would. She so badly wants a child to raise, and I, being the younger of us, have a better chance of being accepted. Why am I hesitating? I used to love being with Cameron, but do I want to enter into the kind of commitment that raising a child entails? No, no, no! With a child, I might not be able to finish at the university. And the world seems to be changing ...* She undid her ponytail and let her long, black hair fall loosely onto her shoulders. She shook her head, letting her hair swish emphatically.

Katie's assistant handed her a card. Katie read it and sighed. She slumped momentarily and then straightened her spine. "The writer asks: 'Why are no white babies being born? Have you discriminated against the white race?'"

With a trace of anger in her voice, Katie answered, "I had hoped that the word 'race' would exit the vocabulary before I died, but I guess it wasn't to be. From the beginning, we made every effort not to discriminate against African Americans and Latinas, and to ensure that the healthiest and brightest women in these groups had the same chance as Anglos, or European Americans, to receive sperm. You probably know that, even before the GSV and the Great Disaster, Anglos were no longer the majority here in Greater Los Angeles. Most of the sperm in the banks, however, was the sperm of Anglo men."

Angela noticed a very tall woman standing at the entrance and scanning the audience. *Is she looking for someone? Or looking for a vacant seat?* In case it was the latter, Angela moved over a seat and motioned to the now-empty seat on the aisle. The woman nodded her thanks, slid into the seat, and scrunched down.

"From the beginning," Katie continued, "we made a deliberate decision both here and on the East Coast that 'people of color'—a euphemistic phrase from the Civil Rights movement of a hundred years ago—should get priority for Anglo or so-called Caucasian sperm. This was to protect the unborn children. We were afraid that visible minorities would suffer more than others in the difficult days that we predicted lay ahead. So African American and Latino sperm went to Anglo applicants, and vice versa, with the smaller amounts of Asian sperm mixed in. If you apply now, as has been the custom since the beginning, you will be told that you have no choice as to the physical characteristics of the donor.

"Look around the room—aren't most of you some *café-au-lait* complexion? I feel pleased that we have achieved a virtually raceless society at the same time that we were preserving our species. I might add that, with the amount of ultraviolet rays hitting the planet today, having a Caucasian complexion is a major health risk. You should see the hats and veils my housemates make me put on before I'm allowed to venture out of doors!

"My grandmother, Lisa Kendall, was one of the Wise Old Women who signed the position paper that led to this policy. Grandmother Lisa was born in 1922 and moved from the North to viciously segregated Mississippi when she was about ten. She was so appalled at the treatment of the black people there that she imagined a solution. It was born of a child's naïveté about grownups and sex: people should be allowed to have a child only with someone of the exact opposite pedigree—pure black with pure white, three-quarters black with three-quarters white, and so on. This way, in one generation, everyone in Mississippi under age thirty would be half and half! (There were no Hispanics or Asians in 1933 Mississippi to complicate her formulas.) The one grown-up to whom she confided her solution was so shocked that Lisa didn't tell anyone else. Also, she told me, she never figured out how this could be achieved voluntarily."

The audience tittered at this. Angela glanced around the auditorium—several whispered conversations had begun, and many hastily scribbled notes were being passed. She looked up at Katie, who seemed to be thoroughly enjoying the reaction Lisa's story had caused.

Angela considered her own dilemma further. *Since I'm darker than most in the audience, maybe I'd have a better chance at getting some sperm. Should I go for it? Could I even receive some of that Anglo-Nobel-Prize sperm? Is Katie reading my mind?*

"You've probably heard," Katie resumed, "about the large and very popular collection of sperm from Nobel Prize winners. One difficulty we had with artificial insemination long before the advent of GSV was that some men, out of a sense of ego, perhaps, were more than generous in their donations to sperm banks—and possibly elsewhere, also." Angela giggled at this, and many in the audience laughed quite loudly. She noticed that the woman beside her had slid down even further into her seat.

"There were a number of cases in the United States in which unwitting half brother and half sister met, were attracted to one another, and conceived a child. Sometimes, unfortunate genes were transmitted in duplicate along with the desired genes for intelligence or athletic prowess or whatever. So we have to be very careful about to whom we give any of this high-donor sperm—this is why everyone's genealogy is so thoroughly documented and why all births must be registered. I'm sure you all learned in school about Mendel and his wrinkled peas and smooth peas, so no lecture here about genetics.

"One high-donor collection was destroyed. The donor had been a physician who secretly impregnated many of his fertility patients and, for obvious reasons, did not keep good records of this practice. Therefore, it was almost impossible to discover his possible daughters and rule them out as recipients for his sperm. Additionally, he had several traits that really did not need to be reproduced in our survival society. I see a hand with a card. Let me guess … No, that was the only collection that was destroyed. Typically, sperm had been donated by very nice men who were facing surgery or going to war and wanted to be sure that they could father a child later on. Or, in some cases, university students donated their sperm to the nonprofit sperm banks for a small remuneration. That's where most of our Asian sperm comes from.

"One personal anecdote here … Before my uncle Ralph went off to the navy, he donated some of his sperm at Grandmother Lisa's request. He was killed in his first month of duty, but his genes live on in many, many people. I wonder, do any of you here have Ralph K. sperm in your ancestry?"

Quite a number of hands went up. Katie was obviously pleased. "Quite a few! Hello, cousins!" She blew kisses toward the audience.

"I understand that he was a very fine fellow who loved children, loved adventure and loved the ocean.

Angela surreptitiously appraised the latecomer. *She sure can't get any lower in her seat ... that must be really uncomfortable with those long legs. Is she hiding from someone? Why a turtleneck sweater in this hot weather? And bare feet? Really big feet! And is that dirt on her face?*

"I was also," Katie continued, "part of a team that went to investigate what was happening with the sperm banks in the American Midwest. We discovered a very distressing situation. All of the sperm samples in that part of the United States had been destroyed by a group of religious fundamentalists who were convinced that the End Days had begun. They believed that God had spoken to them and had told them that the sperm was evil—only after it had been destroyed could they partake in the Rapture.

"Our group made the mistake of visiting a rather large commune of women that was headed by a twenty-five-year-old man who called himself a prophet. He believed that he was to be spared the virus until the time of the Rapture, but, just in case he *should* die, he commanded his harem to kill themselves afterwards. We tried to talk to some of the women—to tell them about the new society we were creating and how they could be a part of it. The preacher caught us, however, and gave us a choice: either be initiated into his cult or face immediate execution. We pretended to accept the first alternative but managed to escape that night, before any of us were forced to undergo his initiation.

"Now for the second very important early decision. Even though it was just the older men who were dying at first, we biologists and physicians feared—and were later proven correct—that the younger men would eventually succumb as well. So it was essential that women be taught the skills of certain occupations that previously had been either exclusively or primarily filled by men—those involved with the operation of oil rigs, telephone systems, sewage-treatment plants, electricity-generating plants, and so on—while there was still time. Many wonderful men refused to go into isolation and used their last days to share their knowledge with us. For example, my almost-husband Peter was an expert on Internet servers. He held training programs that were attended by women from all over the United States. His protégée Roberta was responsible for the speedy creation of our regional Internet here in Southern California.

"I'm wondering ... do any of you have uncles or fathers or grandfathers who stayed out in the world to help train women? What were their occupations?"

Several women raised their hands. Katie pointed to one of them, who stood as an assistant quickly provided her with a handheld microphone. The young woman said proudly, "My grandfather knew a lot about how the telephone exchanges worked. When he was a younger man, he had been a telephone lineman—the kind that climbed the poles to fix the wires when there had been a storm. My mother told me that he taught a whole lot of women everything he knew. He lived a lot longer than most men his age. Mom thought that he just refused to die until he got this training finished." She sat down as Katie and the audience applauded.

Katie next pointed to someone she knew. "Jo, how about you?"

"My uncle Joe was a really good auto mechanic," Jo said "He taught my mother everything he knew. She worked with him until he died and then took over his shop. Mom is retired now, but she taught the trade to me and my sister, so the shop is now called Jo and Marie's Auto Repair. We're here in Westwood, open for business." Again, the audience applauded, and many waved hello to Jo.

Katie nodded to a middle-aged woman dressed in surgical greens. "I'd like to pay tribute to a very wonderful surgeon, Dr. Samuel Hershkowitz. He was no relation to me, but he stayed out to train many women in his exceptional techniques. One of these women trained me. And ..." She turned toward the first woman who spoke. "... like your grandfather, he lived a lot longer than average for his age group."

"I knew your Dr. Hershkowitz," Katie said. "He performed surgery on my hand when I was a child, and it's still in great shape!" She held up her hand and rotated it to demonstrate. "We are very grateful to all of these men, and to you women for telling us about them. Maybe we can hear from the rest of you in the dining-hall during the break."

She continued with her lecture. "The United States, Canada, Europe, Australia, New Zealand—these places were at least semi-ready for the Gender-Specific Virus. They boasted large numbers of university-educated women, many of whom had already entered traditionally male occupations. This, however, was not the case in Africa, the Middle East, most of Latin America, and parts of Asia. Those parts of the globe are presumed to be virtually uninhabited today.

"In the United States, we can thank the Civil Rights Bill of 1964—nearly twenty years before I was born—for its part in creating a generation of educated and assertive women. This law mandated equal rights for *all* minorities, including women. The incorporation of gender into the bill had resulted from an amendment attached to it by a representative from the South, which was still feeling threatened by the Supreme Court decision in *Brown v. Board of Education,* ten years earlier, that racially-segregated public schools violated the Fourteenth Amendment. Howard Smith, a perennial congressman from Virginia, had thought that his amendment would insure the defeat of the Civil Rights Bill.

"He was wrong! As a result, women were no longer prevented from entering certain professions or learning certain skills. And so, when the Gender-Specific Virus emerged, there were women prepared to take over the jobs that in my grandmother's day had been performed by men only.

"Grandmother Lisa took to her grave the injustice she had felt when, even though she had been the top student in her premed class, she was denied entrance to medical school after Pearl Harbor. The medical recruiter from the navy told her, 'We aren't taking any *girls*. Don't you know there's a war going on?' In contrast, when I got my PhD in biology, more than half of my classmates were women. And there was no gender hiring bias by the labs, medical schools, and universities.

"Before we stop for our break, I'll answer a few questions I've been given about the first part of the lecture. One woman asks: 'What caused some men to die quickly and others to last longer?' That's a wonderful question and the answer is that we really don't know. We never could do the studies in time and get the data in the usual scientific way.

"Why not? Well, there was no large-scale longitudinal study of men in progress from which we could crunch the data to see if there were any significant variables that identified the early mortalities. The morgues were far too busy to get in-depth case histories on the deceased. So we are left only with hypotheses.

"The one that I find most compelling is that it was the angry men who had died first—that the anger had depleted their adrenal glands, which left them more vulnerable. I should warn you that I have a personal and emotional reason for holding with this hypothesis. My father, who was one of the angriest men I ever knew—he hated all people who weren't of English ancestry—was one of the first of the men to die here in Los Angeles. I also like the hypothesis implied here in the stories of Dr. Hershkowitz and the telephone expert." Katie gave an appreciative nod toward the latter man's granddaughter. "Perhaps having a mission to complete had some sort of protective effect on those who lasted longer.

"Here's another question: 'What do you miss most about the Old Days?' The men, of course! It still seems unnatural to never see men anywhere. My dreams frequently include groups of men as they were in the Old Days. Then I wake up with such a feeling of loss. And, yes, I miss Peter in particular. We had both assumed that we would be together for the rest of our lives."

Angela held her breath as Katie seemed to choke up, spreading her elbows onto the lectern and lowering her head. But she quickly raised her head again and smiled ruefully at her audience, as if in acknowledgment of her momentary weakness. Angela breathed again and realized that she had instinctively half stood up, as if to go to Katie's rescue. She sat back down and noticed that the eyes of the tall woman next to her were as moist as her own.

"I also miss dogs," Katie continued. "How many of you have ever had a dog as a pet? Only a few hands—I'm guessing that you women are old enough to remember the years before the Great Disaster. How many of you have never petted a dog?" Most hands were raised. "I'm so sorry that you've never had a dog for a pet. Our cats are wonderful animals; without them, we would probably be overrun with rats. But you don't get the devoted adoration from a cat that we used to get from our dogs.

"Let me give you a brief list of things I *don't* miss. First, the traffic! You probably can't imagine how clogged those wide and now useless freeways were at certain times of the day. Most of the huge gas-burning vehicles on the roads were occupied by a single person, and they often traveled no faster than a person could go on her bike!

"I don't miss road rage. I'm happy that I need to define the phrase for you. Some motorists would get so angry at other drivers who were perhaps going too slowly or who had cut in front of them that they would express their displeasure on the freeway. They would honk their horns or tailgate or curse—or even shoot and kill the driver who had enraged them.

"I don't miss processed food. We, with our homegrown food, are a much healthier group of people than those folks back at the turn of the century, who consumed foods filled with chemicals.

"I also don't miss a society in which an old person could die in his or her apartment and remain unnoticed until neighbors were alerted by the odor. I'll have some more to say about that after the break. But now—orange juice and some raw snacks in the next room. Twenty minutes."

During the Break

There was the usual commotion—people leaving their seats, moving out of the hall, everyone talking at once. Angela waited for the tall woman to leave their row first, but the woman instead turned to Angela and asked, in a soft voice, "Can I talk to you?"

"Sure."

"Do you go to the university?"

"Yes, I do."

"What are you studying?"

"History, like Katie's grandmother. Are you at the U?"

"No. I want to go, but I'm not sure they'll take me."

"Why wouldn't they?"

"Well, I was homeschooled, and I know that there must be a lot that my mother never taught me that I probably would have learned in a real school."

"Homeschooled? Then ... you must be ..." Angela felt confused by a new sensation. Her cheeks flushed and grew warm.

"That's right. My name is Teddy." He guardedly pulled down his turtleneck to reveal what Angela knew to be an "Adam's apple" from pictures she had seen.

"Oh, my goodness," Angela exclaimed. "So *that's* why you sat so hunched-down." She looked around to see that most people had already left the auditorium. No one was paying any attention to them. "You don't want to be noticed, right? Are you afraid of the virus?"

"No, not the virus. I've never been out of my commune before, and I don't really know how to act in the world. I've never known another man, so I don't know how men are supposed to behave. The women in the commune always treated me differently than they treated one another. There were lots of secrets that they never shared with me."

Angela was now facing Teddy directly. "Damn," she said, "that must have been hard on you! Where is your commune? What kind is it? Oh, excuse me ... my name is Angela." She held out her hand to Teddy.

Teddy smiled at her as he took her hand, holding it rather than just shaking it. "I like that name," he said. Angela got that same warm feeling again. "I come from a farming commune in Pendleton."

"Pendleton? That's a long way from here. A hundred miles?"

Teddy nodded.

"How on earth did you get here?" Angela asked as she gently reclaimed her hand.

"I started walking three days ago, but I got lucky and got a ride part of the way with a veggiemobile, and then a scooter." Teddy's eyes lit up as he remembered the journey. "People were really nice. They saw me walking and stopped to ask if I wanted a ride. Is that customary?"

"Yes, indeed," Angela answered. There aren't that many veggiemobiles, and bio-fuel is still expensive, so if there's room in their car, people will usually offer to give you a lift. Especially if you're elderly or look tired, or ..." She glanced down at Teddy's feet. "You were were walking barefooted? All the way from Pendleton?"

Teddy smiled sheepishly. "Yeah. They hid my shoes. I guess they thought it would stop me from coming to this lecture. I have twelve mothers, but none has been to the university, and they don't think I need to go, either."

Angela felt indignant. "Teddy," she said forcefully, "you've *got* to tell Katie all this on a comment card! She'll know how to help you."

"You call her Katie like you know her!" Teddy sounded surprised and somehow wistful.

"Everyone knows Katie. She's been everyone's favorite biology and genetics teacher for the last fifty years. My friend Cameron is the great-granddaughter of Lisa Kendall's sister-in-law. Those two women and Katie's father owned three fairly large houses on the same block. They've since merged into a sort of compound for university faculty and students. I have a bed in Lisa Kendall's History House, and Katie lives next door in her father's old house, which is more or less the Biology House. There's a lot of running back and forth among the three of them. Group picnics and so on, too."

Angela was very aware that she had referred to Cameron as her "friend," not as her partner. *What's going on with me?* she wondered. *Why am I more comfortable with this strange new man-creature than I am with Cameron? Is it because he's not bossy, and she is?*

After the Break

Both Teddy and Angela became aware that people were filtering back into the auditorium. They broke eye contact, settled back into their seats, and busied themselves with books and papers. Without looking at Teddy, Angela passed him a comment card—she guessed that he had not known to pick up a card or two at the entrance to the auditorium. Teddy smiled his thanks and started writing on the card.

With his eyes no longer on her, Angela felt free to look at Teddy more objectively. *His hair is so straight and so black—even blacker than my own! Such a large head and such strong features ... How in the world could I have not guessed that this was a man? I've never known a woman with such large and powerful hands.*

Katie approached the lectern and looked serenely out at the audience. When the conversational buzz had stopped, she resumed her lecture. "Before I get started on the Great Disaster, there are three questions I would like to answer. The first: 'Was the virus man-made?' That was an early hypothesis, because we knew there had been some effort as early as the Nixon administration to create a virus that was race-specific. Thankfully, no one succeeded with that heinous experiment. And no, we have no evidence that GSV was man-made. Its origin, however, is still quite mysterious.

"The second question: 'What progress has been made on either finding a vaccine for the GSV or somehow getting boy babies to survive longer?' There have been three lines of research. The obvious one was to isolate the virus, map out its DNA, and reverse engineer a remedial drug and a vaccine. All of this took time, and it was twenty years before we could develop a drug that we thought would work. However, the male children who received the drug did not live as long as the control group. So the drug was destroyed, and a research group has been searching for another ever since.

"The second research line involved cloning. Of course, this wouldn't produce any male children, but the Council thought that it might be a good interim measure until we could find a way to have our male children live longer. Furthermore, if we had no success with the males, we thought that cloning would be a good way to produce female children after our supplies of sperm had run out. I'm sure everyone here knows what a terrible disaster it turned out to be. It was a devastating emotional experience for the mothers who raised these clones.

"But the third line of research is showing great promise. We postulated that there must be a protective gene on the X chromosome that causes women to be immune to the GSV. Its absence on the Y chromosome could cause men to succumb to the GSV. So we started tinkering with the Y in random samples of sperm, adding various different genes from the X chromosome. We ended up with three different kinds of amended Y chromosome sperm. Twenty-one years ago, we started using them experimentally. In 5 percent of inseminations, we used Y-amended sperm mixed with an equal amount of X sperm from the same donor. Since the results were very good, ten years later, 50 percent of the inseminations were with the Y-amended sperm. For the last seven years, we have used *only* Y-amended sperm.

So far, the female children in the experimental groups have been just as healthy as those in the control group. The really good news is that the male children are far outliving those in the control group. In fact, the rate of male deaths in the experimental group is about the same as it was in the Old Days. Therefore, we feel reasonably certain that all male babies born from now on will be immune to the GSV. We have received sperm donations from all males conceived using the first group of amended sperm, but we won't start using it until after we have reviewed the progress of a few children who have been conceived in the old-fashioned way."

Angela gasped. A myriad of whispered conversations started all over the hall. Katie was amused and waited them out. "Yes, we are all very hopeful that we are on the right track. Time will tell which of our three chromosome reconstructions will be the most viable—or maybe all three will be useful." Angela looked over at Teddy. He had stopped writing and was staring straight ahead. He had slouched down in his seat again.

"And this brings me to the third question. 'You say that you believe that men will start living longer and will come out of hiding. What will that be like?'"

"I think that will depend on us, on how we welcome them into our society. Will we recognize our common humanity and rejoice in having a two-gender society once again? Or will we view their reappearance as an intrusion into our new way of living? Throughout human history, people have been only too ready to label people who are different from the majority as 'The Other.' They have ostracized, exploited, or persecuted them. In the twentieth century, the Jews in Germany, the African-Americans in the United States, and the Palestinian Arabs in Israel all suffered this fate. I hope it won't happen here.

"Some women, remembering the accounts of how badly women were treated by men in some previous societies, may want revenge. Let's be on guard against that impulse. We will need to be sensitive to how vulnerable our men will feel on leaving isolation, emerging from a protected environment, and coming into the world. We can be caring teachers and guides, or we can be arrogant know-it-alls who refuse to share knowledge or positions of influence."

Teddy and Angela glanced at each other. They smiled together in unspoken agreement with Katie's last comments.

"Since we are now using Y-amended sperm for all inseminations, in thirty years, our population under thirty years old will most likely be half male and half female, as in the Old Days. Actually, if the old ratio holds, there will be a slightly larger number of males. When we are certain that the GSV does not pose a threat to these Y-amended fellows, we can stop the custom of homeschooling and let them go to regular schools. These boys will not have to suffer the deprivation and isolation that boys have endured for the last fifty years. That means that you younger people here—your generation—will be the transition generation. It's really up to you what our society will be like thirty years from now."

Teddy and Angela again sought each other's eyes. They nodded their agreement with Katie's words.

"And now, we come to sex. Heterosexual sex will rear its very lovely head. This is going to be a big learning experience for all concerned. We will need to remember what we learned in our all-female society—that coerced sex is culturally incorrect. Not all women will be interested in having a sexual relationship with a man. And that's just as well—initially, there won't be enough men to go around! In the Old Days, about 10 percent of women were lesbians. As a biologist, I suspect that same percentage will hold true when other options for sexual pleasure become available."

Teddy hesitantly glanced at Angela. Embarrassed, she first kept her gaze on Katie and then looked down at her hands in her lap.

"Now ... the Great Disaster. People in my grandmother's generation all had very clear memories of where they were and what they were doing in 1963 when they heard the news of President Kennedy's assassination. Similarly, all of us in my generation have our stories of the shock of the World Trade Center's demolition in 2001, as well as of the Great Disaster in 2010. This is my story:

"Two weeks before the Disaster, teams of biologists and physicians from Boston and New York left on fact-finding missions to South America and Africa. I was on the South American team. We wanted to see whether the survival rate of the men in indigenous communities was any better than that in our urban and developed communities. If so, what was their secret? Well, it wasn't any better there. In fact, it was worse. In some places, there weren't even any young boys. We brought a significant quantity of sperm to donate, but it was summarily rejected by the natives, who were very suspicious of our motives.

"Our group left some sperm in Buenos Aires and Caracas, the two communities that we judged were best equipped for survival. The African team saw only limited hope for Cape Town and Johannesburg—the AIDS pandemic on that continent had complicated matters considerably. They cut their trip short and returned to the United States before the Great Disaster. We shared our preliminary findings with each other as our tours progressed. But, of course, we never got to see their final report.

"You may be thinking that we were being very generous with a very precious commodity. Not really. We didn't bring with us any sperm that had been donated *before* the virus appeared. It was all sperm that had been donated by surviving younger men in the weeks preceding our trips. For all we knew, this sperm could have been carrying the virus. Peter was a donor who made a large contribution."

Angela glanced over at Teddy. He was still writing on his card, now on the back side and in very small print. She wrote on her card, "Katie, please help this fellow. I think he had to run away from his commune. They took away his shoes to keep him from leaving." She signed her name. When Teddy had finished writing, she took his card, paper clipped it to hers, stood, and waved them until an assistant came to collect them.

"At one level," Katie continued briskly, "it had been a great honor to be chosen to be on one of these teams at my young age. At another level, it wasn't—we were considered expendable. The trips were pretty iffy—we had no guarantees about airport-control conditions, and we didn't even know if we could get our planes refueled. Peter didn't want me to go; we had some black humor about which one of us would die first. I telephoned and e-mailed him whenever I could. He joked that he was taking notes, so as to be able to make my report for me if I didn't make it back.

"We had an adventure at the end of our trip that was only too reminiscent of that earlier misadventure in the Plains States. We visited an Indian village deep in the Ecuadorian jungle. Now, these weren't the Spanish-speaking Indians who wove rugs and made pottery for the tourist trade near Quito. These folks had little commerce with mainstream Ecuador, much less with people from outside the country. We arrived at a very bad time. The last of their males had just died, and the women were involved in an elaborate ritual of mourning. They indicated that we must stay and join them in the ceremonies, which went on for three days.

"The interpreter we had brought with us from Quito didn't understand the language very well and became quite hysterical; she was sure that the ritual would culminate in a human sacrifice—and that would most likely be us. Three women in our eight-member team were European Americans, and the Indians seemed offended or repelled by our white faces. But they were appeased when we applied mud-packs and covered up our whiteness.

"Carmen, a Latina team member who looked more like our hostesses than our interpreter did, became the mediator of choice. It was she who had suggested the mud packs. After the Indians had exhausted themselves with dancing and chanting and drinking and drumming, they permitted us to leave, but not before we had given away all our watches, wedding rings, bracelets, and lockets. One woman asked me for my ponytail ribbons.

"We soon made it back to our plane, where our anxious pilot was waiting. In our absence, she had heard some very scary stories about the area we were visiting. She had been listening to weather reports from all over. 'Cumbre Vieja is erupting,' she told us. We all looked at her blankly. 'It's a volcano in the Canary Islands.'

"'They're off the coast of Morocco, but they belong to Spain,' she added, when this group of scientists seemed to be geographically-challenged. She related to us a worst-case scenario she had once read about. An eruption fifty years earlier had created a fissure on the western slope of the volcano. Another eruption could cause the whole western side of the island to cascade into the ocean, which could create a mega-tsunami.

"We were all unimpressed with this bit of trivia. We were eager to get aboard and go home, and we were still congratulating ourselves on having emerged alive from the jungle. But our pilot continued, 'If this should happen, Boston and New York airports would be hit with waves of thirty meters or higher. I may be an alarmist, but I've changed the destination of our flight plan to Los Angeles. Any objections?'

"We asked about the National Weather Bureau and the Department of Homeland Security—what did they say?

"Our pilot answered, 'Homeland Security says not to worry. Tsunamis happen in the Pacific and Indian Oceans, not the Atlantic.'

"Our collective response was to go to Los Angeles, if this was the best answer that Homeland Security could give. This was only a few years after the not-too-stellar performance of FEMA and Homeland Security when Hurricane Katrina hit New Orleans and the Gulf Coast. The only one of us who demurred was Carmen, who had been hoping to make it home in time for her daughter's *quinceañera*.

"We had time to make a few phone calls. My first was to Maria Hernandez, the head of the Genetics Committee here in Los Angeles. She wasn't in, so I left a message explaining that our plane was being diverted to Los Angeles and that I would need some overnight refrigeration of sperm and blood samples.

"No one was home at my mother's house in L.A., either, so I just left a message asking if I could spend the night. I didn't ask for lodging for my colleagues, as I felt that would have been pushing the envelope a bit. My mother and I were not on friendly terms—she blamed me and Peter for my father's death. She believed that Peter had given Dad the virus on a visit we had made in the fall of 2007. Ironically, my father had been demanding that we come, so that he could meet 'that Greek boy' that I was planning to marry! Mother had been so angry that she'd had my sister call me to say that I wasn't welcome at the funeral. Yes, Dad had died early enough that there was a regular funeral—a grave was dug, and he was buried. Later, of course, there wouldn't be enough womanpower to dig graves, and mass cremations would be held on the beaches, instead.

"Thank goodness, I was able to reach Peter before we left Quito. He was upset because our plane had been due back in Boston two days earlier, and he hadn't heard from me in several days. I explained our delay and regaled him with our adventure in the jungle. I told him of our pilot's concern about a tsunami and asked what people were saying in Boston. He replied that yes, the volcano was erupting, but Homeland Security was saying not to worry—that tsunamis happened in the Pacific, but never in the Atlantic. No evacuation had been ordered. My response was that if Homeland Security said not to worry, it was time to head for the hills.

"'Another Katrina, you think?' Peter asked. CNN had covered *that* disaster around the clock, and we had watched it unfold together. I answered him, 'Seriously, Peter, why don't you take the dog and go up to the White Mountains for a few days?' He said that he would, but he had to wind up the current workshop first. The pilot was tugging at my sleeve, so we had to say good-bye. That was the last time I ever spoke to Peter."

Katie paused for a sip of water. Several people in the audience were covertly drying a few tears.

"On the plane, we scoured the radio dial for reports on Cumbre Vieja. After we had been in the air for an hour, it happened. The whole western side of the volcano slid into the ocean. It was a volume of land larger than the Isle of Man, they said. This broadcast was from England, which had taken the possibility of a tsunami more seriously than had the United States and had ordered an evacuation of London and the coast. Within minutes, it seemed, the tsunami hit the other islands in the Canaries, and then Morocco and the Western Sahara. Next was the coast of Portugal.

"Three hours later, the tsunami hit Plymouth and the south coast of Ireland with what the BBC was estimating to be thirty-meter waves. A short time later, they were reporting that London's financial district was under water and that the tsunami was headed up the Thames estuary. But the main force of the tsunami was headed westward, traveling at the speed of a jet airplane. Landfall on the Atlantic coast would be in about an hour, in Newfoundland.

"We sat in shock waiting for the next blow, although we did think to thank our prescient pilot. Carmen was crying, and I comforted her. We both knew that Boston would be next, but I was holding on to a mental picture of Peter and the dog up in the mountains. Finally, we got some U.S. news. It seemed that FEMA had sprung into action only after hearing that the tsunami had completely inundated Lisbon, killing tens of thousands of people. After the landslide, the Portuguese had had only a two-hour window of opportunity to evacuate. Swiss and French planes filmed the tsunami surging inland, up the Tagus River.

"Then FEMA ordered an evacuation of the entire Atlantic coast. Finally! But we feared that it would be too late for many people. There were major traffic jams accompanied by road rage on all the highways leading out of the major cities—Boston, New York, Philadelphia, Baltimore, Washington, and Miami. FEMA reported that the waves could be as high as seventy-five feet when they hit. This was a considerable underestimation, as it turned out.

"Then the tsunami hit the United States. The radio from New York was estimating that the waves that hit Boston were as high as one hundred and fifty feet. The tsunami surged up both the Charles and Mystic Rivers; Harvard and MIT were inundated to an estimated depth of thirty feet or so. The announcer was saying that authorities doubted that Harvard's historic old brick buildings could survive. We looked at one another—there go our laboratories. And maybe also our sperm banks. I was trying to remember their elevations and hoping for the best.

"The New York radio went dead when the tsunami hit Manhattan. The Atlanta radio valiantly tried to record what was happening in New York, Washington—and then Florida, which became completely flooded. Even fragile New Orleans was hit, although the landfall on Florida's east coast had absorbed a lot of the force, and the waves were '*only* hurricane-size in Louisiana,' they said.

"Finally, our twelve-hour flight was over, and we landed at Santa Monica airport. Maria Hernandez was there with all the equipment we needed to preserve our sperm and blood samples. Grandmother Lisa was there, too. She told me, 'You're coming home with me. And bring any of your team who need a place to stay.' They all accepted, and we piled into Maria's truck and Lisa's car. And that was how the original Biology House came to be.

"We didn't know then that one of the first things Maria had done after she got the message from me was to call Lisa, and that the two of them had gone out and bought mattresses, sheets, and towels for the whole planeload of us. At that point, we thought that we would be staying for just a few days, and then we would fly home to Boston. Maria and Lisa didn't disillusion us then, but bustled around running tubs and getting people settled. Carmen and I took turns at the telephone and computer trying to reach her daughter, Peter, and the families of the others on our team.

"After Carmen gave up and went to bed, I found a list of local ham-radio operators and obsessively telephoned each of them asking that they send messages to Peter and Carmen's daughter. The bad news was that they were hearing from only a few people in a few isolated communities. And there were hordes of people like me on the West Coast, frantically trying to reach family and businesses in the East. 'I think we're going to have to write off New York and Washington,' one of the ham operators told me. 'Probably Boston, too.'

"Grandmother Lisa came to find me and asked me how long it had been since I'd had a full night's sleep or a bath. She had a tub of hot water ready for me, filled almost to the top. We hadn't yet learned to conserve water and fuel!

"I told her what the ham operator had said. Lisa answered, 'I'm afraid he's right. I'm very grateful to your pilot for changing course. We're going to need you here in LA.' She put me to bed with her white poodle, AbigailAdams. I drank the herbal tea she had brewed and fell asleep hugging Abby.

"When I woke up ten hours later, I could see that Lisa, Maria, and some other older women had been busy. Long before anyone else, they had realized that we were going to be on our own in Los Angeles. Soon, there would be no cash coming out of those money-machines called ATMs, and people would realize that their money was worthless, anyway. The financial centers of London, New York, and Amsterdam had all been destroyed by the mega-tsunami. There would soon be no trucks hauling food and gasoline, so they knew that we would have to provide for the equitable distribution of what we had here.

"As a committee, they went to the LA City Hall and convinced the mayor that no more deliveries of gasoline should be made to service-station pumps. The bulk of the supply should be reserved for fire engines, ambulances, and other high-priority vehicles. They also thought that electricity might have to be rationed—limited to a certain number of hours per day—until we had further developed alternative energy sources.

"A group of far-sighted physicians was also there with plans to commandeer and sequester all supplies of narcotics, antibiotics, and hypodermic needles—much as we had taken over the sperm banks only a few years before. Lisa was concerned about what people would eat until they learned to grow their own food. She had traveled a lot in Mexico and Central America and was impressed at how healthy people were on their inexpensive staple diet of rice, corn, and beans, so she suggested that these commodities be taken from all the food markets and be made freely available to everyone. And they had done all this while I was still asleep!

"This group of women soon became known as the 'Wise Old Women'—most of them were in their late fifties or older—and they evolved into what we know today as the Council. That day, they agreed that we would of necessity become a barter society, but could not decide how the change should be accomplished, or whether it should be regulated by some central authority. As it turned out, the barter system developed spontaneously.

"I saw one of the first signs as I bicycled to the U that first morning. There was a woman named Elsa who owned a large house on a rather large plot of land that was encircled by a tall stone wall. Elsa had plastered over a section of these decorative stones to make a billboard. On it, she had painted: 'Have tomatoes, need lettuce and avocadoes.' Her security gate, which had always been kept shut in all the years I had lived near this home, was wide open. Her request was quite obviously answered—within a week, there was a new sign, which read: 'Salad at 5. All welcome. Bring additions or just come and eat.' Elsa invited other gardeners to share her home, and together they raised bumper crops. The house soon became an unofficial neighborhood center.

"Other such billboards began appearing on houses, apartment buildings, and lawns. After Roberta got the local Internet running, craigslist.com was revived. Yes, craigslist antedates both the GSV and the Great Disaster. Craig was a San Francisco programmer who had created the list back before the Millennium as a free announcement board to get the word out about everyday, real-world stuff—landlords with empty apartments, people looking to rent, folks with stuff to sell or give away, and so on.

"Our neighborhood health-delivery system may have gotten started when the first 'Nurse Practitioner Here' sign appeared on a home. There had been no conscious design on anyone's part, as far as I know, to draw on the Cuban model of neighborhood clinics, which had been known to work so well—but this is what happened, and it is still working well here, as you know.

"Looking back, I am still amazed and more than a little proud of how well we behaved in this crisis—of how we developed a cooperative society, as opposed to a competitive one. We heard rumors of different outcomes in the middle states and in the surviving pockets on the East Coast—violence, armed robberies, shootings, and so on. Perhaps hearing those stories made us decide to do it differently? We had several built-in advantages. First of all, there was our climate. We have a long growing season and can grow just about everything. Then, Southern California had been warned for so long to be ready for 'The Big One'—a huge earthquake—that most homes already had supplies of canned goods, water, batteries for flashlights, and so on.

"We were also more environmentally conscious than many other localities. Many homes had solar panels, and many people were already growing food to make sure that their veggies were organic. There were lots of hybrid-engine cars and scooters. We had forests of wind turbines, and some people had already experimented with biofuels and the conversion of regular cars to run on biofuel. These women immediately came forward with offers to create veggiemobiles. Converting scooters to biofuel was even simpler, and scooters, bikes, and just plain walking became the most common methods of getting from one place to another.

"Cell phones quit working almost at once, but local landline telephones continued to work, and women had been trained in their maintenance. A few local radio stations and one TV channel continued to operate and were used for community announcements. All commercial advertising ceased—that's another thing that I don't miss! The national networks based in New York City ceased operating immediately; CNN in Atlanta hung in there for a while before it, too, faded away.

"It was soon apparent that most of the chain stores in LA had been owned by out-of-state corporations, which would neither be making any new deliveries nor coming to collect their profits. Radio and TV advised people to eat up the contents of their refrigerators and freezers, as electricity could soon be reduced to a few hours a day. Grocery stores put up signs inviting people to come and take from their freezers what they and their neighbors could consume that evening. The store managers were all young women fairly recently appointed to their jobs upon the death or retirement of the male managers. History has not recorded which woman and which store had the idea first, but the practice soon spread to the entire community.

"The manager of another kind of store had a similar thought. She ran a branch of a nationwide hardware and nursery chain. She opened a portion of her store and gave away spades, pickaxes, sacks of soil, seeds, and plants to anyone who would promise to start a home food-garden. And again, the word got around, and other outside-owned nurseries had similar giveaways.

"And then there was the question of community size. There was a British economist named Fritz Schumacher, who had written one of Lisa's favorite books, *Small is Beautiful: Economics as if People Mattered.* In it, he postulated that a population of five hundred thousand is about the upper limit for a city if its inhabitants are to have any meaningful input—if the city is to be a democracy. We had lost more than two-thirds of our population in the course of just a few years. With the new constraints on transportation and communication, our various neighborhoods—Pasadena, Santa Monica, Brentwood, Whittier, and so on—shrank until they contained much fewer than a half-million people apiece, and so became more responsive to community ideas and complaints.

"Don't misunderstand me here. I am *not* saying that it was a blessing that all those people died. Far from it. But there were some benefits from having an attenuated population. A major one, of course, was that we staved off the worst effects of global warming. Before GSV and the Great Disaster, experts had been saying that the planet was at the tipping point.

"It's time to give this eighty-year-old voice a break. But first, I've received a question that I want to answer. The card reads: 'I am a man of nineteen. I live in a farming commune near Pendleton. I want to leave and go to the U. Can you help me?' He signs himself 'Teddy.'"

Angela was very aware that Katie had read only a small portion of Teddy's card. She also noticed the buzz in the auditorium and the turning of heads. Women were trying to locate Teddy in the audience.

"Teddy," Katie said, "you sound like someone who should definitely be at the university. See me after the lecture. You can stay at my commune tonight, and I'll take you to the U tomorrow."

Katie scanned the audience for Angela and Teddy. "Or, better yet," she said, "there seem to be a lot of women curious to see what a man looks like. Would you be willing to come up on the stage and say hello to them?"

Teddy tried to slither even further down into his seat; Angela stood and prodded him to go forward. Teddy saw a sea of faces turn toward him, their eyes devouring him. He grabbed Angela's hand and pulled her behind him as he raced down the long aisle toward the stage.

Katie held fast to the lectern for balance. This young man who was running toward her with Angela in tow looked like a reincarnated Peter! Where had he come from? She resolved to keep her emotions and her confusion under control.

Teddy rushed up the steps and then hesitated several feet from the lectern. The stage lights blinded him, and he wondered what to do next. Katie detached the microphone from the stand and moved toward him.

She held out her hand to him. "Hello, Teddy! I'm Katie, and I'm very pleased to meet you. Thanks for coming up to the stage."

Teddy stepped forward and grasped her hand as if for support. Its warmth and Katie's welcome calmed him, but he was still feeling nervous. She tilted the microphone toward him, and he spoke into it rather nervously. "Yes, ma'am. I'm pleased to meet you, too."

"Teddy, would you like to tell the audience what you grow on your commune?"

Teddy, feeling a little more comfortable, let go of Angela's hand, but he kept his eyes on Katie as he answered, "Beans and corn. Lots of beans and corn! And many other vegetables, too. And some specialty things, like Stevia."

"And what do you think you would like to study at the U?"

Teddy shot a quick glance at the audience before answering. "I don't know. There are so many things I don't know. I like to take things apart and put them back together again. So maybe engineering. I don't know."

Many hands in the audience were waving cards. One of them, Angela noticed, was Cameron's friend Brandy, in the second row.

"Of course you don't know yet," said Katie reassuringly. "Tomorrow, we'll start helping you discover what fits. Maybe a first-semester schedule with a little of this and a little of that." She addressed the audience: "But now, a break. Snacks in the next room. Twenty minutes."

Room 232, Roberts Hall

Katie deftly maneuvered Teddy and Angela to the back of the stage before any women in the audience could reach them. She led them down a hall at a fast clip to a seminar room that was sometimes used for an overflow audience from the auditorium. It was furnished with couches and chairs arranged for conversational groups.

Katie didn't take the time to sit down. "Thank you, Angela, my dear. Teddy, you chose a lucky seat this morning. Angela is a very caring and practical person."

Teddy nodded.

Katie got right to the point. "Now, Teddy, where exactly is your commune, and what is the name of your birth mother?"

"It's in Pendleton. I think it was a marine base in the Old Days. My mother's name was Mary—I never knew her last name."

"Hm, well, that's a start," said Katie. "Sorry, kids, I've got to go. But I'll be back!" She smiled at them and, as she neared the door, said, "Angela, you might want to keep this door locked." With that, Katie swiftly left the room, her cane seeming to propel her into a faster gait.

Angela and Teddy looked at one another, both of them curious and self-conscious. They headed for the longest couch and sat down.

Teddy broke the silence. "I sure learned a lot today; I never knew all that about the Great Disaster. Did you?"

Angela didn't really look at Teddy as she answered. "Some of Katie's story was new to me—the part about her trip to South America and the people in the jungle. But we learned all about the Great Disaster in school. We had geography lessons just like in the Old Days, so that we would be prepared for when the world opened up and we could travel again."

Teddy sighed. "I don't think any of my mothers have a notion of where any of those places are. We were pretty isolated."

Angela turned to face him, ready with some questions that she had been dying to ask. "How did you ever find out about this lecture, then? I see you have a flyer."

"Domenica gave it to me. She was my contact with the outside world. She came to the commune every two weeks or so with her truck, bringing supplies and taking away crops. I used to help her load and unload, and we would talk. She told me a lot about what it was like outside. She said that she had seen a few men lately, and she thought that it was safe now and rather urged me to leave the place."

"So then what happened? You told me they hid your shoes."

"It caused quite a commotion when I told them at supper that I'd like to go to this lecture. Big Mama—the woman who runs the place—laughed at me. She asked if I had any idea how far away UCLA was and said that I'd never get here. To placate her, I agreed that it was a crazy idea. Then one of the other women told Big Mama how I'd been talking about wanting to enroll at the university. Big Mama said that this was out of the question.

"That night, just after I fell asleep, I heard someone come into my room and then leave. I waited a few minutes, then got up and realized that she had taken my only pair of shoes. Most likely, it was Lupe, Big Mama's current girlfriend. That did it! I packed all my extra clothes in this bag, stole down to the kitchen, swiped a lot of bread and cheese, filled a jug with water, and left."

"That was very brave of you," Angela said.

"Impulsive, not brave. And I'm afraid I've made a big mistake." Teddy looked away from Angela as he spoke. "I left a little girl behind—my daughter, Solana. I was so angry, I didn't think of what might happen to her before I could come back for her."

"Teddy! You have a daughter?" Angela was taken aback.

Teddy looked at Angela almost pleadingly. "She is so pretty and so smart. She loves to draw pictures. I think that she might grow up to be an artist, like her grandmother. I love her so much!" He lowered his arms and head down to his knees and sobbed. Angela slid over and put an arm around him. He turned, buried his face in her shoulder, and continued to weep.

Angela soothed him as she spoke. "We'll have to tell Katie about Solana. She'll want to get her out of the commune."

Teddy raised his head and quickly wiped his eyes. He was excited now. "Really? You think Katie could rescue Solana? I told her about Solana on my comment card."

"Well, the Genetics Committee makes a point of keeping track of all new babies, and I'll bet that you've never had a visit from the Committee."

"No, we didn't. They come to see all the new babies?"

"Yes, or else the mothers bring the babies in. And then the children get a checkup at one year, three years, six years—I don't remember the exact schedule. The check-ups are to help the Genetics Committee to determine which sperm are healthiest, and which maybe shouldn't be used any more. So Solana has never been checked? Or her birth registered?"

"No, never. Nor was I. I was born there, in the commune."

Angela was incredulous. "Was there a visiting health practitioner or a midwife? For you, or for Solana?"

"Nope. Big Mama says that she was a nurse before she started the commune, and she's always taken care of anyone who got sick or who hurt themselves in the field. She was the midwife for Solana—and I guess for me, too. I never asked Mary." Teddy was obviously uncomfortable at revealing the commune's unorthodox customs.

Angela felt that she should change the subject. "Tell me about Mary. You said she was an artist."

Teddy opened his pack and pulled out a drawing. "I snatched two of her drawings when I was packing. This is me when I was about Solana's age."

Angela examined the drawing of a laughing four-year-old boy who was showing someone his toy truck. "You were a beautiful little kid," she said. "And you look very happy here."

"I don't remember her drawing that, but I'm guessing that she'd been playing with me not long before. We had great times together; she played with me every minute of her free time. That truck was my favorite toy."

"Did you have many toys?"

"A lot more than you'd imagine. The Marine Corps must have left the base in a big hurry—they left a lot of stuff behind. We broke into the boarded-up houses that were on our parcel of land and found all sorts of useful things. That's where I found men's shoes and clothes after I got bigger." Teddy became quite animated. "Best of all were the books in English that we found!"

"Really? What kind of books?"

"A lot of novels—some of them were written a really long time ago, like *Moby Dick*—quite a bit of science fiction, some detective stories … Some of them were printed on cheap paper that had gotten so yellow that they were a struggle to read. The best-preserved were the textbooks. Mary had taught me arithmetic and algebra before she died. I learned trigonometry and calculus from the books."

Angela clapped her hands. "That's outstanding, Teddy! What else?"

"Well, there was an old atlas, so *I* know where Ecuador and the Canary Islands are!" They laughed. "Then a basic history of the United States up to the 1960s, three volumes of what must have been a fifteen-volume encyclopedia, and textbooks on chemistry and engineering."

"You read them all?"

"Every word. The mothers thought I was crazy, but there wasn't much else to do in our free time. I got tired of watching the old movies on television. It made more sense to read the books."

"That basic history of the United States … was it written by Charles and Mary Beard?"

It was Teddy's turn to clap. "How did you guess?"

"It was a very popular book—it probably sold a million copies, and was considered a very good standard history. But it must have left you wondering what came next."

Teddy nodded. "That's right, but not for long. The best haul of books was hidden in a closet under some sheets—a bunch of books written by people who hated presidents like Nixon and Reagan and Bush. Both Bushes. Those books filled in some of the gaps. But I want to hear about *you* … what *your* life is like."

It was easier for Angela to be the questioner than the confider, but she answered as best she could. "Well, as I told you, I'm a history major here at the U. Before that, I lived with my mother Cindy in a commune with three other girls close to me in age, and their mothers. It was like having sisters; we had loads of fun together—going to the beach, helping each other with homework, and so on. I loved school, especially history and geography. I had a pretty happy childhood."

"Not a single unhappy moment?"

Angela hesitated. "Well … we had a little brother who died when he was four. We'd known that he might not live to be very old, but it was still very sad. Evvie and I were the ones who found him … in the morning, when we went in to get him up and dressed for breakfast. His mother was on the night shift."

Teddy put his hand on Angela's arm. "That must have been really hard on you. How old were you?"

"Thirteen."

"That's the age I was when Mary died."

"Were you the one who found her?"

"Well … we knew that she was dying. I'd been sitting up with her all night holding her hand, and she just stopped breathing."

"Oh, Teddy …" Angela stopped short at the sound of Katie's voice, piped into the room from the auditorium.

"Most of your questions have to do with Teddy," Katie said. "Some of you are annoyed that I whisked him away."

"Not me!" Teddy laughed.

Not me, either, thought Angela.

"I can certainly appreciate your interest," Katie continued, "and your curiosity to know more about him. But coming here has been a rather overwhelming experience for him. Until a few days ago, he had never been outside his commune, and he hadn't met more than twenty people in his life. It was very brave of him to come up on stage …" Angela clapped her hands and grinned at Teddy. "… and I was not going to risk having him badgered with questions." And now Teddy clapped.

"You all will be meeting more and more young men," said Katie. "I hope that you will be sensitive to their rather special circumstances.

"Now … where did I leave off? I think I was trying to explain how we succeeded in creating a survival society while many other communities, as far as we know, failed. It was partly due to generational factors. Lisa's and Maria's generations—they were born in 1922 and 1935, respectively—and my own, were mostly able to meet the challenge. The generations in between—filled with people like my mother—typically went to pieces. When there were no more twenty-dollar bills emerging magically from those money machines called ATMs, when they realized that all their investments were just so much paper, they acted as though there were nothing left to live for. And, indeed, many of them committed suicide. They had been born after the Second World War, in a time of escalating prosperity. Their parents had showered them with all the luxuries that they themselves, having been children during the Great Depression and a world war, had not known. And so, my parents' generation grew up with a sense of entitlement. Psychologically, many were quite unprepared for the two shocks of GSV and the Atlantic Tsunami.

"My generation, on the other hand, had come along at a time when there was no longer a guaranteed promise of good times forever. There was the increasingly realized threat of global warming. There was the frustration with a government that was as unresponsive to the climatic threat as they were to the wishes and needs of the majority—a government that had started and perpetuated illegal wars against sovereign nations. Gas prices had risen so high that many people had to make major changes in their lifestyles—moving closer to work or enduring much longer commutes on trains and buses and so on.

"The dollar, which had been the world's *de facto* exchange currency since the end of the Second World War, had given way to the euro when two major oil-producing countries announced that they would be selling oil for euros instead of dollars. Then, some of the creditors of the massive debt that the United States had accumulated started asking for their money back. The *quid pro quo* arrangement of the United States borrowing money from China so that American consumers could afford to buy Chinese manufactured goods began to collapse. The country was very close to bankruptcy when the Great Disaster settled matters for us. For my generation, it seemed almost a relief to be free of all these threats and to have the energy to get to work and create something different and better.

"From the very beginning, there were spontaneous efforts to see that no one was left without friends, food, and shelter. People with large homes—like Elsa—invited others in to live and share food and tasks. Apartment buildings held weekly meetings for all residents; there was a collective responsibility to see that the elderly and disabled were being cared for. In the exceptionally hot summer before the Great Disaster, there had been several cases of people dying in their apartments, their absence unnoticed until the odor of rotting flesh alerted the neighbors. We were determined to see that things like this would not happen in our new society.

"I can't emphasize enough how this all came about organically. Alerted by some innovative folks who put up signs on wallboards, people gathered in churches, synagogues, community centers, high-school auditoriums—any central spot within a bike-ride or an easy walk of their homes—to discuss ideas, needs, resource availability, and so on. Without anyone putting a label on what we were doing, we quickly moved from being a group of individuals to being participants in community building.

"In our discussions, we stressed that, in our desire to see that resources were shared equitably, we did not want to make the mistakes that had been made by the central command structures of the communist countries during much of the twentieth century. I remember someone at my neighborhood meeting ridiculing the practice in the Soviet Union of micro-managing from a distance and with no input from the local people—how in the world could Moscow know how much toilet paper Vladivostok would need for the following year?"

Angela and Teddy giggled at this remark.

"With the exception of the four things I have already mentioned—sperm distribution, gasoline storage, the stockpiling of essential medical supplies, and the impoundment of basic food supplies—the Council of Greater Los Angeles made no autocratic decisions. Their role then and since has been that of an information center and an agency for the implementation of area-wide projects suggested by neighborhood committees and individuals—the desalinization project, for example.

"An interesting suggestion was made by a majority of the neighborhoods in the first decade after the Great Disaster. They didn't want their daughters taught only in English, as our sister societies to the north—Santa Barbara, San Francisco, Portland, and Seattle—were doing. We here in Los Angeles and in San Diego had much larger populations of Spanish-speaking people. It was feared that, although our children might all emerge with similar complexions, we could still develop a class society based on proficiency in English and which language was the mother tongue. So, for a few years, we had two kinds of schools for the youngsters: Spanish-immersion for girls whose home language was English and English-immersion for those whose first language was Spanish. The Asian mothers were free to choose whichever language they wanted for their daughters, and virtually all of them chose English. There was just one kind of high school, as now, with both languages being used in the classroom.

"But, after a few years, that experiment didn't seem like such a good one, as it schooled the two language groups separately in the lower grades. We definitely didn't want segregation to foster the creation of gangs, which had been such a problem before GSV. So, again at the request of the neighborhood committees and after taking into consideration statements from individuals on their Evaluation Cards, the experiment was ended. Afterward, there was one kind of primary school, which used Spanish for half the day and English for the other half.

"San Diego still uses the immersion system for the lower grades. Shortly after we in Los Angeles abandoned the immersion program, Greater San Diego expanded to include Baja California and part of the west coast of Mexico. One of the first things that happened in that area after the Great Disaster was the abandonment of any semblance of border control. The Mexicans needed American sperm, and we needed their expertise at growing those staple crops of beans, corn, and rice. This resulted in an exchange in which everyone won.

Teddy interjected here: "Most of the women in the commune had mothers who came from Mexico. They preferred to speak in Spanish, but Mary always spoke to me in English."

"She sounds very different from the other women," said Angela.

"Yes, she was."

They resumed listening to Katie's lecture.

"Another border was dissolved in the north. The Seattle and Vancouver communities became close partners. The Canadian dollar was still being used, and that became the medium of exchange instead of the barter scrip that evolved along the rest of the West Coast. Here in Los Angeles, again at the request of the neighborhood groups, the Council started printing 'uren,' with the idea that an hour spent teaching children should be the equivalent of an hour spent picking beans. I don't know who suggested that we use the Dutch word for 'hour,' but it sounded different enough from 'hour' and '*hora*' to avoid any linguistic confusion.

"Now, back to my own personal story. I woke up from my long and restful sleep to find that some elf had washed and dried all my dirty clothes. No one was around, so I dressed, hopped on the bike that Lisa had said I should use, and set off for the genetics department at the U. On the way, I noticed the sign on Elsa's garden wall. That gave me such a feeling of hope.

"Maria was there, obviously expecting me. She asked me to join the others of my team in writing the report of our trip to Latin America. After I finished that, Maria told me that there was a job waiting for me in the virology department. I demurred—said that I didn't know much about viruses and that my experience was with sperm banks and the evaluation of sperm recipients. Surely they would want to continue with that work!

"Maria assured me that I could get up to speed in virology in no time, and she talked about the urgent need to find a vaccine or a cure for GSV. She said that I had been ideal for the recipient-evaluation job in Boston, but not here in LA. It might have proved too difficult for me, she said, to be objective about the distribution of my Uncle Ralph's sperm, to say nothing of Peter's.

"Little did she know—or maybe she guessed?—that I had been secretly planning to get myself inseminated with Peter's sperm. This, of course, would have been a flagrant violation of the policy that I had been instrumental in promoting! For about six months, I held onto the fantasy of somehow having Peter's child. It was my way of handling my loss. Maria softened the blow of my grief by inviting me to the monthly genetics colloquium meetings. Actually, I never left the Genetics Committee, as the research path that I chose was the third one—the experiments to amend the Y chromosome—which not only fit my academic training, but also seemed to me to offer the most hopeful prospects.

"Well, I think that's a crazy rule!" Teddy said indignantly. "Katie should have been allowed to have Peter's sperm."

"I agree with you," said Angela. "Some people get so hung up on the rules that they forget about the people. So what if the kid turned out looking more white than most? He or she would have been darker than Katie, anyway, because Peter was Greek. In the end, though, I suppose that Katie has mothered several generations of students, including me."

"And so," Katie continued, "I began what became my life's work—the reconstruction of the Y chromosome. I won't bore you with a description of the many wrong paths we took. Our team became very close to one another. Our brainstorming sessions were great fun. No idea was deemed too preposterous to consider. In fact, one of the three accepted solutions emerged from an idea that was pretty crazy, but that we kept coming back to.

"Carmen joined us after a few months. By exaggerating the depth of her friendship with Peter, she had convinced Maria that she shouldn't be a member of the team that evaluated sperm recipients. In fact, I think she had met him only once or twice. Carmen and I hadn't known each other very well in the Boston days. I had always liked and respected her, and I had been happy that she'd agreed to be on the team that had gone to Latin America. After that trip, my admiration for her expertise and

her interpersonal skills knew no bounds. Remember, she was the one who had nego-
tiated our safe departure from the jungle. We roomed together in Lisa's house and
worked on our grief together. Eventually, our deep friendship evolved into—I'm sure
you've guessed it by now, if you didn't already know—a loving partnership that
lasted until her death fifteen years ago." Katie paused.

"Did you know Carmen?" Teddy asked Angela.

"No. She died long before I moved to the compound. I've heard Katie talk about
her a lot, though."

Katie had resumed speaking. "A few months after the Great Disaster, my mother
died. Hers was one of the more melodramatic suicides. She drove off a cliff into the
ocean in a newly converted veggiemobile. Such a selfish thing to do!" Katie shook her
head.

"Carmen and I moved into her house to look after my little sister, who was pretty
unstable. Susie had always been neurotically attached to our mother, and had
dropped out of the U after Dad died. Despite our best efforts to cheer her up, get her
interested in life, and find some work that would engage her, she continued to disin-
tegrate. One day, we came home from the lab, and Susie was gone. She had just disappeared and was never found. Carmen guessed that she had walked into the ocean
near the wreck of my mother's car. If so, her body never washed up.

"After that, some members of our team and some biologists from next door
moved into Dad's house. We hung up a sign reading 'Biology House.' Lisa filled up
the empty beds with historians and hung up her own sign: 'History House.' They've
been repainted a few times, but those same signs are still there. It's reassuring to have
some sense of continuity even though, as the Buddha assured us, all is change.

"And there is another change coming. Not just the reintroduction of men and
boys into our society, but another possible change that some of the neighborhood
meetings are discussing. We have been aware all along, thanks to ham radio, of other
pockets of survivors in the old United States. We know which of them exist and
which have died out. In the early days, we were too concerned with our own survival
to reach out and offer any assistance. Lately, however, we have been communicating
with people in Chicago and Atlanta—two communities that had well-stocked sperm
banks. We have, of course, given them the protocols for amending the Y chromosome.

"Both communities have asked for visits from West Coast scientists. Seattle is
making plans to send a convoy of vehicles to Chicago in the near future. We are talking about putting together a similar convoy for Atlanta. This would be a much more
difficult undertaking—it's a longer distance, for one thing. Could we carry enough
biofuel and other provisions to get us there? There are long stretches of uninhabited

desert, so it should probably be a spring or fall trip. There will be roads and bridges that haven't been repaired for fifty years. We have been promised enough biofuel for the return trip, but … It sounds as iffy as our trip to Latin America. However, if I were younger—a lot younger—I would definitely volunteer! I'm so curious to see exactly how they've constructed *their* new society. The ham operators have tried to tell us … but can a fish adequately describe living in water?"

"Wow!" Teddy said to Angela. "This is exciting! Would you like to go on the Atlanta trip?"

Angela shook her head. "No, I want to stay here and finish at the U, and then get a PhD."

"How many years will all that take?"

"It depends on how fast you can write and do research. I've already started on my dissertation."

"Do you have a title?" Teddy asked.

"Yes!" Angela said proudly. "*The United States, 1910–2010: Progressivism and the New Deal vs. Dreams of Empire.*"

"That's something I'd like to read!" said Teddy.

"My guess," Katie continued, "is that the Atlanta trip won't happen until after we've heard the results of the Chicago trip. And, of course, we must have community consensus on the project. Now, I'll answer a few final questions before we get to that birthday cake and ice cream.

"This writer asks, 'Are we ever going to have a democracy again? Or is the Council always going to be making the important decisions for the rest of us?' To begin with, I would quibble with the word 'again.' The United States before the GSV was a republic, but it wasn't really a democracy. In those days, a senator from Wyoming representing half a million people had the same vote in the Senate as a senator from California representing thirty-six million. That's a multiple of over seventy!

"After the Great Disaster, we didn't have the structure to continue the old system of political parties, candidates, and voting. Instead, as you know, every year, on the first Sunday in November—in the Old Days, voting was always held on a Tuesday, which disenfranchised a lot of working people—we have Evaluation Day. Whoever wishes to participate can go to her neighborhood headquarters, sign in, and be given a card on which she can check either 'Yes, I approve of most of the Council's decisions and would like them to continue for another year,' or 'No, I am not in agreement with most of the Council's decisions and want some major changes made.'"

Teddy turned to Angela and admitted, "None of us ever voted on Evaluation Day. I knew about it from the TV, of course, and from Domenica, but I had no idea where our neighborhood center was, or even if we had one."

"You were living in Greater San Diego. Maybe they're not as civic minded as we are." The two of them were sprawled on opposite ends of the couch, looking at one another as they listened to Katie.

"This may sound like the way people voted for Stalin in the old Soviet Union," Katie went on, "but that's not true in the case of Greater Los Angeles. Stalin always got a 97 percent or better approval rating; the Council has never received above 80 percent, but never less than 55 percent. The most important part of the Evaluation Card is the space at the bottom where women, regardless of how they have voted, are asked for suggestions, criticisms, evaluations of current Council members, and nominations for new Council members. The Council takes these notes very seriously and has acted on many of them. I was on the Council myself for a number of years, and I can vouch for that.

"Also, keep in mind that the Council *doesn't* make the important decisions. The four exceptions that I mentioned earlier were made in the early days and were crucial ones; we might not have survived without them. Incidentally, the turnout on Evaluation Day has always been much greater than the turnout for voting in the last years of the Old Days. So, which society has been more democratic?

"The Council is preparing a fairly comprehensive card for Evaluation Day this November. There will be slates of candidates sent in by neighborhood committees for Council seats; there will be numerous questions, such as those dealing with the revision of the barter credits, further extensions of our community, the redevelopment of the cell phone system, outreach to Atlanta, and so on. Again, write down on your cards any ideas or concerns that you may have. And, as always, take your problems and your nominations to your neighborhood committees.

"For those of you who missed my rant in the first part of this lecture, democracy had pretty much disappeared in the old United States in the last decade before GSV. There were two stolen presidential elections. Thanks to the Supreme Court and some shenanigans by election officials in Florida, the 2000 election went to the man Lisa liked to call the 'Selected Resident of the White House.' She always avoided using his name and the word 'president' in the same sentence. Then, in 2004, the election was decided by Ohio, where electronic voting machines had been programmed to fail. I think that our current system—in which a group of people, elected by their neighborhood center, individually record the number of yes and no votes, and then, if their totals don't agree, they do it again—is a lot safer for a democratic process.

"Was she talking about George Bush?" Teddy asked.

"Yes, the second George Bush."

"Another question writer," Katie continued, "seems concerned about authoritarianism. And that's good! We need to be aware of any tendencies in that direction, and resist them. She asks: 'You say there have been some babies conceived in the old-fashioned way. Did the Genetics Committee select the partners?'

Katie laughed. "Most definitely not! And it will not in the future. The Committee hopes, but does not require, that a prospective couple come in for genetic counseling, to rule out consanguinity. A few sperm donors have engendered quite a large number of individuals, so we do need to be cautious. But hey, people will get carried away, and we don't have supplies of condoms and diaphragms and birth control pills, like in the Old Days.

"Birth registration will continue to be required, as in the Old Days. I hope that doesn't sound too fascistic. You people also need to take responsibility for your own genetic counseling. How many of you know the identities of all the sperm donors in your ancestry?"

"So few of you!" Katie's tone made it clear that she was unhappy with the response. "All you have to do is ask at the Registry, and I would suggest that everyone do that.

"And now, for our last question. It's a biggie—but I promised to try to answer them all. 'Since you have had both male and female sexual partners, can you tell us which is better?' This reminds me of the Greek myth about Tiresias. It seems that Zeus and Hera were having one of their domestic quarrels up on Mount Olympus. Zeus was maintaining that women got more pleasure out of sex than men. Hera said, no, no, it was the *men* who had the most fun. To settle this dispute, they called on Tiresias, a mortal who had lived part of his life as a man, and part as a woman. When the question was put to him, he answered, 'Women get more pleasure, of course.' This so enraged Hera that she had him blinded.

"Now, I'm not afraid of being blinded if I unequivocally answer a somewhat similar question, but the *true* answer is that it depends on the psychology of the people involved. While there are various sexual techniques and romantic situations that can enhance the physiological release, let me as a biologist remind you, that 95 percent of sex occurs up here." Katie tapped her head authoritatively. "And it is the quality of *love* that each of you brings to the experience that makes it so ... well, ecstatic!

"And on that sexy note, let's go have some birthday cake and ice cream!"

The loudspeaker in the room where Angela and Teddy sat communicated the rumble of people leaving their seats and the sudden eruption of many conversations.

Angela and Teddy were self-conscious again. After a time, Angela broke the silence. "Teddy, I'm wondering ... it's none of my business, but were you in love with Solana's mother, like Katie was with Peter?"

Teddy shook his head emphatically. "No, not at all! I know that sounds like the arrogant attitude some men were supposed to have had in the Old Days, but the truth is that Big Mama insisted that I sleep with a different woman every month, beginning when I was about fourteen."

Angela gasped. "How awful!"

Teddy chuckled. "What Big Mama never knew was that most of the women didn't *want* to get pregnant—they had other arrangements. So I never had sex with them. Lupe, Solana's mother, rather forced things. How about you? Do you have a partner?"

Angela hesitated, but only briefly. "Yes and no. In the beginning, I thought that I loved Cameron—she's my roommate at History House—but lately, I've been feeling differently, and I don't know how to break it off. She's very domineering—she's demanding that I get inseminated and we that we raise the baby together. I absolutely *don't* want to have a baby, and especially not with her." Angela noticed her new firm attitude on the subject and felt relieved that she had come to a definite decision.

Teddy sounded almost hurt by her statement. "You never want to have a baby?"

"Not until I have my PhD. I'm afraid that a baby would hold me back in my studies. But later, I'd love to have a baby boy like the little brother we lost."

Teddy nodded.

They fell quiet for a while, absorbed in their own thoughts, until Teddy said, "Tell me about cloning. I read about Dolly the sheep, and I think there were other animals, but I never knew that you could clone people."

"The biologists didn't manage to do that until after the Great Disaster, so it wouldn't have been in those books you found at the marine base. The idea was frowned on for ethical reasons, which seemed to disappear pretty quickly when it became a question of keeping our species going! But unfortunately, the clones grew fast, aged quickly, and died young."

Angela thought for a moment. "I thought it was interesting," she said, "that Katie didn't mention in her lecture that she herself had been cloned. I remember her saying once that her clone was so much smarter than she was—the clone had taught herself to read when she was three, whereas Katie herself hadn't learned to read until she went to school at the usual age."

Teddy pondered this new information and then said, "Katie talked about how devastating the experience was for the mothers who had raised the clones. But it must have been just as disturbing to see someone who looked and talked like you—and maybe even thought like you—mature so quickly and then die. Did Katie know her clone? How long did she live?"

"Yes, I think Katie saw her clone on at least five or six different occasions. She was a teenager when she died, but Katie said that she looked like a very old woman."

"That is so tragic."

They fell silent again. Teddy stared into space. Angela marveled at the empathy of this man who certainly had not come from a nurturing environment. *He's probably a wonderful father,* she thought.

"Tell me more about Solana," Angela said.

Teddy was happy to do so. "She's four years old and looks a lot like me. Her first word was 'Daddy,' and I find her waiting for me every evening when I come in from the fields. We play games, and I read to her. We have a few early-reader books left over from my childhood, and we've read them so many times that I think she could recite them from memory. She likes any book that has pictures, even those encyclopedia volumes." The smile left his face. "I doubt that anyone has read to her the last two nights."

"Don't worry, Teddy." Angela tried to sound reassuring. "I know that it's going to be all right."

The loudspeaker now brought in the conversational hubbub from the dining hall. They heard someone exclaim to Katie, "If they ever revive the Nobel Prize, you should get one!"

"That's very kind of you," Katie answered, "but remember that it was a *team* project."

Teddy and Angela couldn't catch what the unknown woman said next, but Katie's next words were clear and decisive. "Excuse me, please, but I see that Maureen is about to leave, and I need to speak to her."

"Katie isn't wasting any time!" Angela laughed.

Teddy was confused. "What do you mean?"

"Maureen is one of her best friends," Angela explained. "She's the current head of the Genetics Committee, and Katie probably wants to tell her about you and Solana and your lack of registration. I'm so glad that you told Katie about Solana on your card."

"What do you think will happen?" Teddy seemed worried.

"Nothing that you need to worry about, but I wouldn't like to be in Big Mama's shoes. Those two women are formidable!"

Later

There was a knock at the door. Both Teddy and Angela jumped up to open it, but Teddy got there first. Katie was standing there holding two dishes of ice cream and wrapped pieces of cake. "I'm sorry all that took so long … you know, speeches and everything."

Teddy took the food from her and murmured his thanks. Katie locked the door and sank into an armchair.

"We heard it all. We think you should get a Nobel Prize, too!"

"Well, thank you. If it's not too rude of me, could I get you to eat your ice cream so that we can get out of here before the crowd discovers where I've stashed you?"

Angela and Teddy dove into the ice cream. Angela was half sitting on one of the arms of an upholstered armchair, and Teddy was more conventionally seated.

"I was able to talk to the head of our Genetics Committee before she left," Katie said, looking at Teddy. "She's going to call the head of the San Diego Genetics Committee tonight, and we'll find out if your birth was ever registered. And also …" Katie hesitated and glanced over at Angela.

"I told Angela about Solana," Teddy said quickly.

Katie seemed pleased. "That's good. Now I don't have to be discreet! I think it's great that you have a daughter, Teddy. She sounds like a lively little person. But from what you said on your card, I doubt that either of your births was registered. That is a major no-no. Solana's birth in particular should have been recorded, as we need to keep very close tabs on all children born of men with Y-amended sperm. You were living in San Diego's jurisdiction, but you and Solana come from LA sperm. So LA has the right to remove you both from San Diego so that we can monitor Solana's progress."

Teddy jumped out of his chair. "That would be wonderful!"

"We need to wait to see what Maureen finds out from San Diego, but she will probably remove Solana from the commune. In that case, I'm going to ask for permission to take Solana home with us and raise her ourselves. Would you like that?"

Teddy was ecstatic. "You mean, we could live at your house?" Katie nodded. "That would be such a relief for me! Oh, Katie, thank you!"

Angela rushed to hug Katie. "What a wonderful idea, Katie. Thank you!"

Katie rose to receive Angela's hug, then turned toward Teddy. He fell into her outstretched arms, where she held him for an extra beat or so before releasing him. She pulled out a handkerchief and dabbed her eyes. "This has been such an emotional day," she excused herself.

Almost immediately, she was businesslike again. "Jo and Chris know that we're in here; they've promised to deflect any prowlers, and they'll collect your dishes." She glanced at their almost-empty ice cream dishes.

"I'll go see if the coast is clear. Then let's all make a dash for my veggiemobile which is at the back of the Hall." Her glance included Angela.

"Thanks," said Angela, "but I have my bike out front."

"Okay, then," Katie said, "but do come to supper tonight, Angela."

Teddy chimed in: "Yes, Angela, please do."

Katie opened the door and peeked down the hall. She beckoned Teddy, who quickly grabbed his slice of cake and waved good-bye to Angela.

Angela stayed behind for a few minutes, finishing her cake and mulling over the afternoon's events.

*   *   *   *

Katie and Teddy made it safely to her car, and they escaped the campus without detection.

"We made it!" Katie giggled like a child who had just pulled a fast one on her parents. She looked over at Teddy, who seemed very somber.

"Teddy, I need to ask you something. I've been so busy for the last few hours, arranging your life for you. But there's a university in San Diego, also. Maybe you would rather go there?"

"No, no, I want to go here. Mary went to UCLA, and she told me what a great university it was. But there's something I need to tell you, and I don't quite know how to say it."

Katie kept her eyes on the road and said, "Don't be scared—just say it!"

"Two of the other mothers are pregnant," Teddy said. "I didn't tell Angela. I was too embarrassed."

Katie's voice held no trace of censure. "I'm so glad you told me! The Genetics Committee will want to remove them from the commune too, since Big Mama doesn't seem to be very trustworthy. Are there any other women who might be pregnant and not know it yet? Any other women you've slept with in the last several months?" Katie sounded almost eager.

"I don't think so. Big Mama made me share my bed with a different woman every month, but the last few didn't want to get pregnant, so we didn't do anything." Teddy felt relieved and was now able to face Katie. "To be honest, I liked having sex with some of them, but I didn't like being *made* to do it. I'd like to be able to choose, and to do it with someone I love … like you said."

Katie chuckled approvingly. "From now on, the choice is yours—and hers. Just check it out first with the Genetics Committee to make sure that you're not already blood relations. We don't have birth control pills any more, and if there are still any condoms or diaphragms around, they're probably all rotten!"

"I read something about a 'rhythm method.'"

Katie laughed. "That was once called 'Roman Catholic Roulette.' The method worked for some women, but not for others. It depended on how regular their menstrual cycles were."

A scooter whizzed past them and tooted.

"That was Chris; she drives a lot faster than I do! We're nearly there."

Minutes later, Katie pulled into the driveway. Virginia was waiting for them at the door.

"Hi, Teddy! I'm Virginia," said the middle-aged woman as she held out her hand to him and turned to Katie. "The whole house is eager to meet him, but I asked them to wait until dinnertime."

"Good thinking, Virginia. That will give Teddy a chance to get cleaned up. I'll look through Dad's old clothes for some shoes."

History House,
Tuesday Evening

Angela bicycled home slowly, dreading the confrontation that was bound to occur and rehearsing what she would say to Cameron. *"Cameron, I'm sorry to disappoint you, but ... "* No! *I'm not sorry, and she* deserves *to be disappointed!* *"Cameron, it was a great lecture, and it made me realize that I definitely don't want to have a baby."* *That's not right, either.* *"Cameron, I am* not *going to have a baby with you!"* Now, *that's more like it! But will I have the courage to say it?*

Before she knew it, she was home. She slipped her bike into its slot and entered the living room she so loved. Most of its walls were lined with books, most of which had belonged to Lisa. The armchairs and couches were old but comfy, strewn with throws to cover the holes in the fraying fabric.

On Angela's way to her room, Mercedes, a fellow history student, whispered to her, "I'm on your side, Angela." With trepidation, Angela continued on to the room she shared with Cameron.

She opened the door. Cameron was waiting for her. Her hands were on her hips, and she was enraged. She had never seemed taller to Angela than she did at this moment. Brandy was at her side, a triumphant smirk on her face.

"I wondered how much longer it would take for you to get home," Cameron snarled. "You were last seen leaving the lecture hall two hours ago. With a man."

"Holding hands," Brandy added nastily.

"Guilty as charged," Angela said. "So ..." Angela stopped talking when she saw what Cameron held in her hands. "What are you doing with my diary? Hand it over!" Angela angrily advanced toward Cameron to grab the book.

Cameron held the diary over her head, far out of Angela's reach. "I was just trying to find out how long you've known this boyfriend of yours."

"*Boyfriend?*" Angela glanced at her watch. "I met him three hours ago! You couldn't wait to ask me? Hand it over!"

Cameron thrust the diary at Angela. "I read enough to know that you don't want us to have a child together. I don't suppose you volunteered for insemination."

Angela clasped the diary to her chest. "That's correct." She looked Cameron up and down, as if seeing her for the first time. *How gawky she is, and how ugly she is when she's angry or not getting her way. Those big red blotches on her face!*

Cameron seemed pleased with Angela's answer—almost triumphant. "Well, Brandy *did* volunteer, and I'd like you to move out right away, so that she can move in."

"If there's any moving out to be done," Angela yelled, "*you* can do it!" She strode around Cameron and Brandy to her bed and threw down her jacket, as though to assert possession of the space. "I was here first, and *I'm* the history major."

"Yeah? Well, *I'm* a Kendall great-granddaughter."

Martha, the head of the House Committee, had arrived at the doorway in time to hear this exchange, and interrupted. "There will be a house meeting at ten tonight to decide who moves and who stays. Meanwhile, Cameron, you and Brandy need to clear out of the room and give Angela a chance to change for dinner. Angela, Katie called to say that dinner will be at seven."

"Yes, go have dinner with your *boyfriend*," was Brandy's parting shot.

Angela was relieved to find that the bathroom at that end of the hall was unoccupied. As she soaped up in the shower, she tried to let go of her anger. *At least it has ended with Cameron,* she thought. Still, some residue of sadness and abandonment remained. She turned on the water and let the tears come—no one could hear her cry here. *This is ridiculous,* she thought, *I'm finally free of Cameron, and I've met a nice new friend, so why am I crying?*

As she made her way through the living room, she saw no sign of either Cameron or Brandy, to her great relief. People were gathering for dinner; many of them waved to her, and all generally looked very friendly. *Maybe I won't be the one to be kicked out,* she thought. Still, the unpleasant sense that had come over her in the shower—the feeling that there was some half-remembered incident that continued to upset her—lingered on.

Biology House, 7 PM

Angela's mood lightened when she entered Katie's living room. It was much larger than the one next door. Angela remembered Katie describing how her mother had had the house rebuilt soon after her marriage, so that it would be bigger and fancier than Lisa's house, and how she had redecorated and bought all-new furniture every two or three years. The room was now full of people who had gathered before dinner.

Teddy was there, and Angela saw that his confidence seemed to have increased many times over. He was surrounded by a half-dozen Biology House women, the whole group laughing and joking. Angela felt a twinge of some emotion that she couldn't name.

Teddy looked so different! The jeans were gone; he was wearing pants with a crease down the front. There was no more turtleneck sweater—instead, he wore a clean white shirt opened at the neck, which framed his Adam's apple. He was wearing shoes, and his long hair had been shorn.

Teddy looked up, saw her, and ran to her side. "You're here! I was afraid you weren't coming." He took her by the hand and brought her into the group. "Angela is my angel," he told them. "She made me write the card to Katie."

Angela felt both relieved and self-conscious as Teddy introduced her to a group that she knew so well. "I like your new clothes," she said. "You look comfortable in them."

An ebullient Teddy stroked the ends of his shirt collar. "They belonged to Katie's father. She says she never throws anything out—you never know when it might come in handy! He was a banker—I'm wearing banker's clothes!" Teddy was highly amused at his new profile. "And these shoes are great! I've never had shoes that fit this well."

Katie came in to call everyone to dinner. She pulled Angela aside and put an arm around her. "I'm sure that History House will vote to keep you," Katie said. "But, if not, we will make a place for you here."

Angela smiled her appreciation. "Thanks, Katie," she said softly. "But I want to stay at History House if I can. I haven't made my way through all of Lisa's books yet!" And she thought, not for the first time, *News sure travels fast in this compound.*

Katie stood at the dining room door, watching as everyone filed down the long buffet table, picked up plates and cutlery, and helped themselves to the different dishes. Teddy was third in line. Katie noticed that he was watching the others and taking his cues from them. *He catches on fast,* she thought approvingly.

Just then, the phone rang. "I'll get it," said Katie. "I'm hoping it's for me." She picked up the receiver in the living room, and, sure enough, it was Maureen.

Maureen was brisk and quickly got to the point of her call. "You were right, Katie. There's no record of either Teddy or Solana at that commune. No record of any child *ever* born there, in fact. San Diego is quite happy to hand both of them over to Los Angeles and didn't question how I knew that LA sperm was involved. What made you think that, anyway?"

"Long story, Maureen," Katie answered. "I'll tell you later. But I have more news! Two of the women at that place are pregnant—by Teddy, of course."

The geneticist in Maureen was jubilant. "That's great! Two more second-generation kids for the database! We'll have to bring those women home with us, too, of course. So we'll need another car. I'll bring mine and meet you there. I told San Diego that we'd arrive at about one or one thirty. Will that fit for you? I know that you're taking Teddy for placement tests in the morning."

Katie was pleased that Maureen's enthusiasm had replaced her curiosity about Teddy's origins. "I think you'd better follow us," Katie said. "Teddy couldn't give exact directions to the farm, and, as I remember, there were several roads leading to the old marine base. Meet us at Testing at around eleven?"

"Okay. And how is Teddy getting along at Biology House?"

"It couldn't be better," Katie said decisively. "The women are enthusiastic about his joining the community.. He's all cleaned up now and has a man's haircut—Virginia's contribution. Barbie Secord was moving out anyway, so I've given him her room. It's small, but there is room for a bed for Solana. Teddy seems to be a devoted father, so I'd recommend that he continue to raise her—with the help of us all at Biology House. Virginia agrees."

"Sounds like a good solution. For now, anyway. See you tomorrow," said Maureen.

Katie returned to the dining room and started filling her plate. The others were already halfway through the meal, and Teddy was returning to the table with a second helping—he clearly hadn't had much to eat for several days.

Everyone looked at Katie, who responded to their unspoken question. "Very good news! Teddy, you, Maureen, and I will be meeting the San Diego genetics people at your commune tomorrow afternoon, and we'll be bringing Solana home with us."

"Thank you, Katie," Teddy murmured, relieved. There were many happy remarks: "I'm so glad that there's going to be a child in this house," and "This is going to be fun!"

Soon, the previous conversational theme had resumed—Teddy had been asking the women about their work.

Virginia, the oldest woman there after Katie, told him, "When I'm not giving young men a haircut, I'm a psychologist. I teach at the U and also see a few people at the Counseling Center. I came here to Biology House a million years ago as a psych student, and I've never left."

"And we are never going to let her leave!" said Eva, who was young and sprightly. "I'm a biology student at the U, and I hope to stay on as a researcher. This is my partner, Sarah."

Sarah affectionately punched Eva's arm and said, "I'm a researcher at the U, and I work with drugs and vaccines. Katie put us out of business—we no longer need an antidote for the GSV. Now we're trying to duplicate one of the effective antibiotic drugs from the Old Days. The formula was a big secret, and, of course, we can't go raid the Patent Office!"

Carolyn, an attractive woman in her midtwenties, spoke next: "I'm a physician. I work at the clinic at the U doing primary-care medicine while I train as an ob-gyn surgeon. My partner is …"

She was interrupted by a husky young woman across the table who raised her hand and said, "Me, Dora! And I don't know a thing about biology—except maybe nutrition."

"She's one of our best cooks!" Eva said.

Dora motioned as if to ward off any further praise, but she smiled at Eva as she continued, "I'm a roofer, too. We keep putting patch after patch on these old roofs. When we finally have to, we install new ones. We also repair the solar panels." She nodded at Chris to her left.

Chris, easily the tallest of the women, looked at Teddy mischievously. "When I'm not guarding doors so that this mysterious new arrival won't be molested," she said, "I repair computers. I'm not a biologist, and I have no partner to introduce. I live out back in what used to be a garage, which is also where I have my repair shop." Embarrassed at having said more than she intended, she turned to the last person to speak.

This was the diminutive Barbie. "I started out as a biology student," she said. Then I got intrigued with writing and the TV community news. I met and fell in love with someone at the studio, and I'm moving in with her. In fact, this is my last night here, and that's my old room you're getting, Teddy. There's a great view of the backyard and the garden."

"But where will you sleep tonight?" Teddy asked immediately.

"One of the living room couches will be fine. Maddy is coming early tomorrow with a veggie to get me and all those bags you may have noticed in the hallway. Her apartment is in Santa Monica."

"We're going to miss you, Barb," Eva said.

"I'll be coming back to see you all—especially Carolyn."

"Tell Teddy your happy news," Eva prompted.

"I'm three months pregnant!"

"Congratulations!" said Teddy. "Having a child is just the greatest experience."

Chris had waited long enough with the questions she had wanted to ask. "Teddy," she said, "I'm really curious to know what it was like for you growing up."

"I'll tell you," Teddy said, "but only if you tell me about your childhood first."

Virginia, the psychologist, intervened. "I have an idea. Let's do a fantasy exercise." All the women nodded assent. Teddy looked around the room, wondering what she was talking about."

"It's okay," Angela said to him. "It's a way to help people remember things, and it facilitates sharing."

"Close your eyes," Virginia said, "and focus on your breathing.... Air coming in, air going out.... Now visualize a big sign in front of you. It has a number on it. The number is the age you are now.... The card flips, and you're one year younger.... It flips again, and you're another year younger. All the way down to fourteen … thirteen … twelve … eleven … ten … nine … *eight*. You are eight years old.... Where are you? … What are you doing? … How are you feeling? … What do you want right now?" All of the participants were now in a half trance. Katie was the first to open her eyes, and she gave Virginia a "thumbs-up."

Virginia waited until a few more of the group had stirred, then continued: "Now open your eyes and write down your experience." She opened a drawer of the buffet and produced some pens and tablets of paper. Teddy guessed that these fantasy exercises must be a common occurrence at Katie's. He quickly started writing.

After most of the group had finished writing, Virginia asked Chris if she would like to go first.

Chris told her story: "It's 2040, and I'm eight years old. I'm in the third grade. I love school, and I love my teacher, but now I'm afraid of her. She's just told us that we must watch the fireworks tonight and then write about them for our homework assignment. I don't *want* to watch another fireworks. I was so scared when that house down the street burned to the ground last year, and so were my two mothers. I rush home to tell them about this awful assignment, and Hannah tells me, 'We have a surprise for you! We're going to the beach to have a picnic supper and to watch the fireworks!' I burst out crying. What is wrong with everyone?

"Ruth puts her arms around me and asks, 'What's the matter?' I tell her I can't bear to see another house burn down. She assures me that this time will be different. 'Trust me. Will you ride with me to the beach on my bike?' I agree, and, of course, she was right. The noise scares me at first, but I love the different explosions and the shooting stars—the ones that look like a comet floating down to earth. I want to find out how these fireworks are made."

There was general laughter and remarks such as, "Chris, just like you to want to know how they're made."

"Excuse me," Teddy said timidly, "but what are fireworks?"

The women seemed to speak all at once. "You must have lived too far out in the country to have seen them—what a pity!" "Let's not tell him; let's surprise him! The next one is only ten days away." "We have them every five years on the anniversary of the Great Disaster, to celebrate our survival."

"May I go next?" Katie asked. "It's 1988, and I'm eight years old. It's a Saturday. I am putting on my jacket. 'Katherine, where are you going?' My mother and father are the only people who call me that, and I hate the name. 'Over to Grandmother Lisa's,' I say. 'You need a jacket to go next door?'" Katie has two very different voices for her eight-year-old self and for her mother. 'She said we might go out to a movie.' 'Well, be back in time for dinner.' 'Yes, Mother.'

"I know—and she knows that I know—that she really doesn't care whether I'm back in time for dinner or not. They'd much rather eat with just Susan, the daughter who never gives them any trouble. Lisa has already packed lunches, along with the signs we made yesterday, into the trunk of her car. Along with Granddaddy Fred, we're off to Simi Valley to picket a man named Oliver North.

"My sign reads, 'You're a bad man, I hope you go to jail.' The crowd is yelling at North as he arrives for his speaking engagement. 'North, North, you're a liar.' We're all having great fun. When we get home, Lisa and Fred drop me off at my door. My parents are waiting for me, and I can see they are all riled up about something. Okay, so I missed dinner, but Lisa called them to say we were eating in Sherman Oaks. But that's not the problem. They saw us on TV. The camera was focused for a while on me and the childish handwriting on my sign. Mother, particularly, is very angry.

"She yells at me. 'What will people think?' I answer her, 'Maybe that someone in this house cares about what is happening in this country and in Nicaragua!' My father yells at me, 'Katherine, don't sass your mother. Go to your room.' I go to my room wishing that I could live with Lisa and Fred instead of these people."

Teddy went next. "I'm eight years old, and I'm living with about twenty women on a farm. I've done a day's work in the fields, and now I can sit at the long table and eat with everyone else. My mother Mary isn't there—she's sick in bed—so I fix an extra plate of food to take to her. Big Mama sees me and says, 'Teddy, what do you think you're doing?' and I say that Mary will be hungry.

"Big Mama says, 'If she's hungry, then she can get up and come to the table like anyone else.' I'm so angry, I feel like hitting her, or at least throwing the plate of food in her face. But I don't. I say, 'Yes, ma'am' and wait until she's out of sight. I take Mary the food and tell her what Big Mama said. Mary says that Big Mama probably thinks that she's dying, and doesn't want to waste food on her.

"This worries me. I don't want my mother Mary to die. Mary tells me that she used to scrounge food for me when I was little, because Big Mama thought that I would die soon of the virus and didn't want to waste the food. I feel so much love for Mary and so much hate for Big Mama. I tell Mary, 'Soon, I'll be bigger, and we'll leave this place.'"

The group was horrified. "Teddy, how awful!" "What a terrible person this Big Mama is!" "Where is Mary now?"

"She died when I was thirteen," Teddy said, "so I never got to take her away from the commune."

Angela stood and put a reassuring hand on Teddy's arm. "May I go next?" she asked. "I have a house meeting in ten minutes." Everyone nodded. "I'm eight years old. It's the middle of the night, and I wake up because I hear my two mothers yelling at one another. I put my hands over my ears because I hate to hear them yelling at each other. It seems to happen almost every night now. Patsy is saying, 'Fine, so *take* Angela! But go. I get to keep the apartment.'

"Cindy answers her: 'We got priority for this apartment because we were having a child, so it seems only reasonable that Angela and I should stay. Patsy yells back: '*We* were having a child? That's a good one. It seems to me that *I* was the one with the swollen belly and the labor pains. I only did it to please you, and look where *that* got me!'

"I cry very softly so they won't hear me. I feel hurt that Patsy doesn't want me, but I'm relieved to finally know which of them is my biological mother and which of them really loves me. Cindy finds us a great commune to live in, and I live there happily with her and some new sisters until I move here to go to the university."

Angela went over to Virginia and hugged her. "Thanks for this exercise. Just what I needed tonight! Sorry that I have to miss hearing the rest of you."

Among the good-bye shouts, several people wished her good luck at her house meeting. *Does* everyone *know?* she wondered.

"Will you come to the University with us tomorrow?" Teddy asked.

Angela looked at Katie. Katie nodded and said, "We leave at eight o'clock."

"Sure thing, Teddy," said Angela.

Back at History House, 9:55 PM

Two of Angela's housemates were waiting for her in the living room. "It's a done deal," Mercedes said. "You're staying, and Cameron is moving into Brandy's place."

Angela glanced at her watch. "But I thought the house meeting would be at ten!"

"There was big argument—a fight, really—at dinner," said Beth, another history major. "Cameron just dared us to kick her out. She said that *you* could move out and go to live with 'that man.' Brandy came close to hitting me when I told Cameron what I thought of her reading your diary. It was getting pretty intense, so Martha told us to change the subject and said that we'd have the house meeting in the living room immediately after dinner. Several of us had heard everything that went on in your room earlier, and we were incensed at the whole bit—especially Cameron reading your diary!"

"The clincher for Martha," Mercedes added, "was Cameron's claim that the room should be hers because she was a Kendall and this had been a Kendall house. Martha told her in no uncertain terms that ancestry ceased to have special privileges fifty years ago."

"Martha wouldn't say—she wanted to spare Cameron the embarrassment, I guess—but we're pretty sure that the vote was unanimous," said Beth. "I'm very happy to have Cameron gone. Sorry, Angela, but I never did like her. I just hope that it's okay with you."

Angela hugged them both. "It's *very* okay with me," she said.

Wednesday Morning, August 18

Katie was bustling around the kitchen when Teddy entered. "Good morning, Teddy! How did you sleep?"

"Very soundly, and from the minute my head hit the pillow. I usually lie awake for a while thinking about my day. But last night, even with so many exciting things to think about, I just conked out! Such a comfortable bed! When I woke up just now and looked around the room, I couldn't believe my luck."

"That's good. I'm fixing breakfast for us both, since this is your first morning here. Usually, each person fixes her own, since we all get up and leave the house at different times. Most of us pack a lunch to take to work or the U. I've put out some fruit for each of us, but you can make your own sandwich. We'll probably eat in the car on the way to Pendleton—it's a good two-hour drive."

"And what about dinner?" Teddy asked as they ate. "The food last night was delicious!"

"I think it was Dora's night. I'd have to look at the bulletin board. Incidentally, she'll be coming with us and doing the driving. As far as dinners are concerned, we take turns cooking. Do you know how to cook?"

Teddy shook his head. "Not really. I used to help Mary after she became the permanent cook for the commune, but we had almost the same food every night—and it was *nothing* like last night."

"Well, we'll put you at the end of the list; that will give you ten days to learn some new recipes. And we have a cookbook. Actually, a number of people use a buddy system and help each other on their cooking nights."

"I'd better find a buddy, then, and fast!"

"There are two other lists. One is for work in the garden, and the other is for the cleaning of the common rooms. Each of us is responsible for cleaning up her own room and the nearest bathroom. I'll show you the bulletin board tonight. Here's Angela, so let's get going!"

In the car, Katie asked Teddy, "Did you have a chance to look at the U catalog last night?"

"Yes, and I must have checked a third of the courses—all sorts of different subjects."

"That's great," said Katie. "It's too late in the school year for you to sign up for courses for credit, but you can audit any class you want."

"And the best part," Katie added, "is that you don't have to keep coming back to the same class. If you find an instructor boring, you can go to a different class the next day."

"Are you more comfortable with Spanish or English?" Katie asked. "Which is your better reading language?"

"English for reading, definitely," Teddy said. "Everyone on the commune likes to speak Spanish, but my mother always spoke to me in English. I was afraid that I might have forgotten how to speak English, but it's all come back to me."

"This gives me a good clue for tracking down your mother's identity," Katie said, "and we'll ask Big Mama for her last name, since Mary avoided telling you. At the U, I'll ask that they give you the English version of the test. But you can write the essays in either English or Spanish—or even Spanglish. Just keep writing whatever comes into your head, and don't worry about the spelling or the grammar."

"I've never taken any kind of test, so …"

"Don't worry," said Katie. "This isn't the kind of test that you pass or fail. It's just to help Admissions know what kinds of things interest you—what you already know, and what you don't yet know, but need to learn."

"I think there must be a lot in that last category," Teddy admitted.

"That's true for all of us, even eighty-year-old me. Incidentally, I noticed you looking at the computers in the library last night. Do you like computers?"

"I don't know; I've never used one. Big Mama had one in her house. I saw it once, when I hauled in some wood for her fireplace, but she wouldn't let me touch it."

"Well, I have a feeling that you're going to love computers. Chris can teach you about the hardware. She builds computers from scavengered parts and keeps all the ones in the neighborhood running. Angela here is very good at the software end and can teach you how to use the essential writing and data-management programs."

"That would be fun!" Angela said. "Come over any evening, and I'll show you the basics. It's too bad we didn't get you started last night—you could have written your essays today on the computer. It's ever so much faster than writing by hand."

"Maybe I could, anyway. I know how to use a typewriter. In fact, I found a broken old one on the base, took it apart, and made it work. The keyboard looks the same."

"I should have thought of that!" Katie said. "We'll find a computer and give you ten minutes with Angela before you go in for the test."

*   *   *   *

"So how did he do on the computer?" Katie asked Angela after Teddy had left for the testing room.

"He's a natural. His spelling and grammar leave a lot to be desired, but aren't *too* bad, considering his lack of schooling. And there's always spell-check!"

"Did you teach it to him?"

"In ten minutes? Katie, he had to know what the green and red underlines were all about. So I told him to just ignore the green—that for the test, nobody would care about grammar and punctuation—but that he might want to change some of the reds. I showed him how to do that with his first sample. He was very quick to recognize the correct spellings on the list."

"Did you print out some samples? Could I see them?"

Angela blushed as she handed the two pages to Katie.
The first one read:

> Anjela I likr you very much and not just becuz you were so kinf nd hlpe me yesterday. You are just a very lovely person and I want to know you better I am glad we will be living nest door to each othet, I want you to meet mi hija Solana. She is very talkative, she tells me that I am her favorite person in all the wold. I make up stories to tell her because there aren't any chilfren'd books in the ommune I felt so sorry about how you and your mother wer treated by that patsy when you were 8. I wanted to hug you but since no one else did it didn't seem like the right thing to do.

Katie read the two copies quickly. "I'm glad you taught him spell-check! Could you do me a favor? Would you have time to run to the library and pick up some children's books before your first class? Thanks! And Angela ... you've never checked out the identities of your sperm donors, right?"

"Never," Angela said.

"Do it," Katie urged. "I think you'll be pleasantly surprised."

Wednesday, 11:15 AM

Teddy was full of enthusiasm as he exited the building and dashed to the car where Katie and Dora were waiting. "That was so much fun! I think I like taking tests! I liked imagining what I would do in all those situations that they described. But some of the forced choices were hard. Which magazine would I rather read: *National Geographic* or *Popular Mechanics?* I wanted to read both of them!"

"So, which did you choose?" Dora asked.

"I think I left that one blank," Teddy said, "thinking to come back to it if I had time. Which would *you* choose?"

"*Popular Mechanics*, definitely. Even though I've never seen either one of them."

A sixtyish Anglo woman with striking auburn hair got out of her nearby car and greeted Katie and Dora affectionately. She held out her hand to Teddy. "Hello, Teddy. So, you're the young man who has the whole community talking! I'm Maureen."

"Good to meet you, Maureen. Thank you for arranging all this." Teddy indicated the three cars assembled behind the Testing Lab.

Katie introduced Teddy and Dora to Keisha and Dawn—younger members of the Genetics Committee who would be traveling with Maureen to Pendleton in the additional two cars—and they set off.

As they drove and ate their lunches, Katie briskly laid out her plan for the day. "I'm not anticipating any trouble with Big Mama—I think we have her outnumbered—but, just in case ... Dora, I want you to stick close to Teddy. Teddy, I want you to find Solana, then go to your room and gather up any important possessions—especially any papers. Then the three of you get into this car and lock it. The rest of us will be having a little talk with Big Mama and the pregnant women. Teddy, where do you think they will be at this time of day?"

"Probably out in the fields or in the kitchen. Supper is usually at five. Neither Solana nor I have many possessions."

"Is she going to miss her mother, do you think?" Katie asked.

"I'm not even sure she knows which woman her mother *is*. Lately, Lupe has been Big Mama's favorite and stays in Big Mama's house, so Solana might even have forgotten all about her by now. Solana is going to be so happy at Biology House—the people there are so eager to meet her! Most of the women at the commune ignore her. Big Mama doesn't like her, and I think that Solana is afraid of Big Mama."

This was an opening for a question that Katie had wanted to ask. "I need to understand more about Big Mama. Why does she do these things—the forced sleeping arrangements, the withholding of food? Is she crazy, or does she like to play God?"

Teddy thought for a moment before answering. "She sure enjoys the power she has over everyone. I think that most of the women are hiding from something and have nowhere else to go. I would sometimes ask them why they didn't leave, and they would just shake their heads without explaining. No one *ever* talked about their childhoods or where they came from. That's why I was so startled by Virginia's exercise last night. But … is Big Mama crazy or playing God? I don't know."

"And Mary … your mother … do you think she was hiding from something?"

"I … Yes, I think she was. Not from anything bad that she had done, mind you. It was more like she was running from some unpleasant situation and then got stuck there at the commune. Having a baby boy and needing to keep him hidden away must have been a problem for her. Some of the women didn't want to be found—they would make sure to stay out of sight whenever Domenica came to the commune. A few did leave from time to time—usually two together, and always in the middle of the night. There used to be as many as twenty women there."

"Did Big Mama get angry when she found out that someone had left?" Katie asked.

Teddy shook his head. "No, oddly enough. She would just shrug and say, 'Good riddance, one less mouth to feed.'"

Dora piped up from the driver's seat. "Are you sure she wasn't murdering them?"

Teddy chuckled. "I'm pretty sure not, although a few of the mothers thought so, and worked even harder in the fields as a result. Except for me and Solana, everyone slept in pretty close quarters with one or two other women, so Big Mama couldn't have pulled off such a thing. How would she dig a grave or two and bury the bodies before daybreak? Big Mama never does a lick of work and is so fat that she can barely move around. Wait 'til you see her!"

"I'm looking forward to it!" said Katie. "But tell me, Teddy, did you never think about running away earlier?"

"Only continually for the last ten years!" Teddy answered. "At first, Mary would always say no because she was afraid that I would catch the virus. Then she got too weak from her lung condition to make a run for it—by this time, she was the permanent cook and didn't work in the fields any more. After she died, Big Mama saw to it that I didn't sleep alone. And after Solana was born, I knew that I had to stay there until she was big enough to leave with me. Domenica told me that she thought she would be able to have the truck one night two months from now and could meet us down the road during a full moon. I hope I didn't make a mistake by leaving too soon—and without Solana."

Dora called to the backseat: "It won't be long now, Teddy. I hope you're watching the road. Be sure to tell me where to turn off for Pendleton."

Teddy paid full attention to the sights along the highway, amazed that they had come so far so quickly. Such a different experience from three days ago!

"Over there!" He pointed out the window to a spot across the highway. "That's where I got my first ride. The sun had just come up."

"Capistrano Beach!" Katie announced excitedly. "Not far now!"

Within minutes, Teddy spotted the entrance road, and Dora turned left into it.

"There's no gate any more," Katie observed. There was only a concrete structure with no doors and no windowpanes. Just beyond that, within sight of the highway, the two cars from the San Diego group were waiting for them.

Dora pulled to a stop, and everyone got out. Maureen introduced them all to Lauren and Hazel from San Diego. Lauren indicated the other two women accompanying them without mentioning their names. "We asked for two women from the Security department, just in case."

Pendleton

The convoy of five veggiemobiles started up the road, with Katie's car in the lead. Dora was driving cautiously, as the once well-paved road had small potholes every twenty feet or so.

"I hope you have a spare tire, Katie!" Dora peered into the rear-view mirror to see if all the cars were following.

Teddy sat next to her and studied a hand-drawn map. "Domenica drew this for me several months ago, and it never left my pocket. I sure needed it to find my way out. I hope it works in reverse."

Katie surveyed the territory beyond her window." This looks familiar. I went to a bike race here when I was a teenager. But it's all hills and rocks—it doesn't look like good farmland."

"It isn't," Teddy said. "We only farm on the few level spots where the Marine Corps built camps. You have to be careful not to go too far beyond that—there's unexploded ordnance all over the place. Big Mama once wanted me to expand the farm too far away from the commune, and I said no, that it was dangerous. She insisted until I told her that the tractor would be destroyed if it hit some ammunition."

"I do not like this woman," Dora said grimly.

"Here! Turn left, Dora." Teddy pointed to a dirt road. The road they had been traveling on continued over a bridge that did not look very safe. Dora turned and drove a short distance up the road. She stopped and waited until she saw that the other four cars had made the turn. They continued slowly. There was a dry riverbed below them to the right. They passed a barely legible sign: "Las Pulgas."

They soon saw some buildings in the distance. From the closest, a weather-beaten wooden shack, an old Taco Bell sign dangled.

"That's the chow hall," said Teddy. He indicated that Dora should turn left onto an even narrower dirt road. He pointed across what might have been an old parade ground to a freshly painted concrete-block house encircled by a forbidding wall. "That's Big Mama's house," he indicated.

"Let's park in front," said Katie.

The other cars drove up and parked alongside Dora. *We've got our troops arrayed in a row, nineteenth-century style*, thought Katie as they got out of the cars.

But no one was in sight. Teddy started to feel very anxious. He could feel the sweat developing in his armpits, and it wasn't a warm day. He looked over at the chow hall, down at the cornfields that occupied most of the former parade ground, over to the four small houses that had not been bulldozed, and then back to Big Mama's house. He saw no one.

Katie, too, was scanning the area. *Except for the rows of corn, it looks like a set for one of those old Westerns*, she thought.

"What now?" Maureen asked.

"Let's get some action here," replied Katie. She leaned on the car horn for several seconds.

She and Maureen had started for the gate to the house when Big Mama emerged from around the wall, waddling as fast as her tremendous thighs would carry her. A far more slender Lupe followed her reluctantly.

"What do you two white-faced women want, and what are you doing on my property?" she demanded.

Before Katie could answer, Big Mama caught sight of Teddy. "So, Teddy, you've come back!" she said triumphantly.

"I've come back for my daughter," said Teddy. "Where is she?"

Big Mama shrugged. "Who knows? She's hiding somewhere. She only sneaks out to scrounge food, the little snitch."

Teddy started running around the commune, yelling Solana's name very loudly. Dora ran beside him, matching him stride for stride. *They look so much alike at a distance,* Katie thought. *In the Old Days, people would have wondered whether Dora was a man or a woman."*

Lauren, the senior of the two San Diego women, approached Big Mama and addressed her. "Ramona Morales, I am Lauren Parrales of the Greater San Diego Council. You have failed to comply with established custom mandated by the Genetics Committee of Greater San Diego to register births. We have failed to find a registration for either that young man, Teddy, or his daughter, Solana. I should warn you that your contract with the San Diego Council to farm this tract is in jeopardy."

"So?" Big Mama spat out the word with disdain.

Katie and Maureen joined Lauren. With a nod from Maureen, Katie joined the attack. "I'm Katie Kendall from the Greater Los Angeles Genetics Committee. Maureen Gabriel and I are here to collect two of your workers, Alicia and Isabella, who are pregnant and, we understand, have not been seen by a health practitioner."

"You can't have them!" said Big Mama. "They're two of my best workers!"

"We're not leaving here without them," Katie said.

"Oh? We'll see about that. Lupe, go get my gun."

"There will be no guns here, except for ours," Lauren said.

The two women from Security whipped pistols from their ankle holsters and approached Lupe. "Okay, Lupe," one of them said, "let's go get that gun. Are there any others?"

Lupe, terrified, answered, "Just one." They prodded her into the house.

Lauren handed Big Mama a tablet of paper and a pen, saying, "I want the names of all the women who live here. Write them down, please."

"Now," she added when Big Mama seemed reluctant. The huge woman resentfully waddled to one of the cars and started writing, using its hood for support.

Katie noticed that five or six workers had appeared and were standing around the edge of the group, keenly interested in what was going on. They were all wearing jeans and long-sleeved shirts. They had probably just come in from the fields. Unfortunately, none of them seemed to be pregnant.

Lauren glanced at the list that Big Mama handed her. "These are just first names. What are their last names?"

"Don't know. They never said, and I never asked."

"Have any of your workers died since you started the commune?" Katie asked.

"One."

"And what was her name?"

"Mary."

"No last name?" Katie persisted.

"Never heard one." Big Mama was still managing to sound defiant, but with increasing difficulty.

"What did you do when she died?" Katie asked in a kinder voice.

"Called downtown. They came and got the body. If they didn't register it, that's not my fault." She glared at Lauren.

Katie was astonished. "But didn't the morticians ask for a last name?"

Ramona shuffled her feet and shrugged. "Yeah ... I made one up."

"Do you remember what name you gave?"

"Might have been Miller."

The two Security women left the house with Lupe. One of them carried a rifle, and she opened the trunk of her car and deposited it there.

Ramona was sagging, physically as well as emotionally. It was obvious that she was not used to standing for any length of time. "I need to sit down," she complained.

Lauren regarded her with contempt. "We are going to take you downtown to see a judge. So you'll be sitting soon." Then she softened a little. "Would you like to get into the car now?"

"Yes."

One of the Security women opened a back door of her car, announced to Ramona that she was being charged with making a threat with a deadly weapon, deftly attached a pair of handcuffs to her wrists, and helped her into the car. There, Big Mama spread out over the entire backseat, her muumuu now up over her knees.

Lupe went to the car's open window and said, "What will I do?"

"You're in charge now," answered Big Mama.

Two of the field-workers looked at one another and, without a word, dashed into Ramona's empty house. The two security guards followed them in.

Katie approached one of the bystanders. "Do you know where we can find Alicia and Isabella?" The woman pointed in the direction of the cornfield, away from the road. "I think they are in the next field," she said.

Teddy and Dora had returned. They hadn't found Solana, and Teddy was distraught. He asked the woman, "Nadia, do you know where Solana is?"

She shook her head. "Sorry, Teddy. I haven't seen her since last night."

Teddy started searching inside the chow-hall, calling out, "Solana, where are you? It's Daddy." Then, as if he were playing a game, he said, "Come out, come out, wherever you are!"

Dora silently joined Teddy in opening closets and looking behind doors.

Katie, Maureen, and the two younger women from the Genetics Committee walked beyond the parade ground, where they started calling out, "Alicia! Isabella!" In a few minutes, they encountered a group of about six women harvesting beans. Two of them were easily identified as pregnant, their very large men's shirts hanging loosely over their unzipped jeans.

"Alicia, Isabella, my name is Maureen Gabriel. I am here from the Los Angeles Genetics Committee. My colleagues and I are concerned that you probably have not seen a doctor or a health practitioner, and you both seem to be pregnant. Is that correct?"

Isabella answered for both of them. "I'm due in two months, and Alicia is due in three, or maybe four."

"And have you seen a doctor or a health practitioner?" Maureen asked.

"No, never, neither one of us," said Isabella.

Maureen spoke in her kindest voice. "That is a big concern for us. You really need to see someone, both for your health and for the health of your unborn children. We came here in several cars today and propose to take you to Los Angeles, where you both can be seen by doctors."

"But what will Big Mama say?" Alicia asked, frightened.

"Big Mama has no say in this."

Isabella was more practical: "And after that?"

"We propose to find you a place to live in Los Angeles until your babies are born. The babies will have to stay in Los Angeles so that the Genetics Committee can monitor their development. You can stay and help to raise them, or you can come back here to live. Or, you might decide that you would rather do some other kind of work instead of farming. If so, we will help you with that."

Isabella seemed jubilant. "¿*Realmente*? We won't have to come back here?"

"No. Just gather up whatever you want to take with you—especially pictures, birth certificates, or any papers that say who you are. Keisha and Dawn will help you," Maureen said, indicating the two younger women. "You will ride back with them, and we will all leave in about fifteen minutes."

"*Gracias*," said Alicia shyly. Isabella took her by the hand, and they walked rapidly to the wooden shack where their rooms were, followed closely by Keisha and Dawn.

"Well, *that* went well," said Maureen. "Keisha and Dawn can interview them on the ride back to LA—find out who they are, how they feel about having a child, what they want to do with the rest of their lives. They both seemed quite happy to leave here, don't you think?"

"Yes," said Katie, "they seemed quite relieved. You handled it well." Katie patted her friend on the arm. "Now, let's find Teddy. I hope he's found Solana."

"I need to talk with Lauren before we leave. I think she's in Big Mama's house. See you in a few minutes." Maureen, well satisfied, dashed away.

*   *   *   *

Teddy and Dora had searched all of the small houses. "Unless she's out in the woods somewhere," Teddy said, "she must be either in the old infirmary or … or in Big Mama's house."

"Oh, Teddy, you don't think …"

"I don't want to think that! Let's try the infirmary first." Teddy was by now thoroughly frightened.

They ran to the infirmary, Teddy again calling out, "Solana, where are you? It's Daddy!" They threw open cupboards and looked in closets. Then Dora put her fingers to her lips. Both of them had heard a soft, "Daddy?" Teddy ran in the direction of the voice, and a very dirty little girl crawled out from behind a stack of musty mattresses.

Teddy lifted her up and started crying. "Solana, are you all right? I'm so sorry I left you!" He brushed a cobweb out of her hair.

"That's all right, Daddy. I knew you would come back." Solana had obviously been crying herself, but now she was trying to comfort Teddy. "Big Mama told me to forget about you ... that I would never see you again ... but I *knew* you would come back!" She held him tightly around the neck.

Then she noticed Dora, who had been quite affected by the reunion and was wiping her eyes. Teddy put Solana down and said, "Solana, this is Dora. She has been helping me look for you. We are going to leave here and go to live in a nice house with Dora and lots of other nice women."

Dora, conscious of her intimidating height, knelt down and held out her arms to Solana. "I'm so glad we found you. We were so scared that something bad had happened to you!"

Solana permitted herself to be hugged by Dora. "Nothing bad happened to me except that I missed my Daddy, and Big Mama was mean to me, and I had to steal food. She called me a useless eater." Solana began to cry.

"My sweet Solana," Teddy said, picking her up again, "we are going where no one will ever call you a nasty name like that. Let's go to our rooms and get all the things that we want to take with us."

He carried Solana out of the infirmary, and Dora followed.

"Where is Big Mama?" Solana asked somewhat anxiously as they neared the shack that had been their home.

Katie had spotted them and heard her question. "The last time I saw her," she answered gleefully, "she had been arrested and was sitting handcuffed in a car, waiting to be taken before a judge in San Diego."

"Well, that's good news!" Teddy said. "Solana, this is Katie. We are going to be living at her house in Los Angeles."

Katie patted Solana's hand. "It's a joy to meet you, Solana. Teddy has been telling us such wonderful things about you. Do you think you would like to come live at my house?"

"Will my daddy be there?"

"Absolutely."

"Then yes, thank you, I would like to come live with you." Solana was very formal with Katie, who was the first white woman she had ever met.

"Let's get our things, Solana," said Teddy, putting her down and taking her by the hand. Katie and Dora followed them to the first house that had been searched. They watched as Solana selected the best of her clothes and discarded the rest. "This is too small," was her verdict on many items. The things she most wanted to take were her crayons, her drawings, *The Cat in the Hat*, and a collection of dried leaves and flowers.

Everyone had their hands full as they went into Teddy's room, where he produced two leather suitcases with stickers from abroad—a hotel in Kyoto, a restaurant in Copenhagen. "These were Mary's suitcases," Teddy said.

"Goodness," Katie said, surprised. "Who do you suppose went to all these places?"

"I asked her about that. She said that someone she knew a long time ago had gone there, but she wouldn't say who."

Teddy relieved the others of their burdens and put them in one of the suitcases. As he rummaged through his closet, Katie reminded him to just bring clothes he really liked. "There are a lot more of Dad's clothes at home that I haven't shown you yet."

Teddy nodded. He gathered up a dozen books, two baseball caps, a Marine Corps jacket, and one gaudy Hawaiian shirt that looked unworn, which he thrust into the second suitcase. Then he reached into the back of the closet and produced a large artist's portfolio.

"This is all that I have of my mother's paintings," he said. "It's my only possession worth keeping, really."

"I'd love to see them after we get home," said Katie.

They walked to Katie's car and stowed the suitcases and portfolio in the trunk. Solana noticed Big Mama in the backseat of the second San Diego car. She pulled Teddy by the hand toward the car for a closer look. Big Mama looked straight ahead, as though they didn't exist.

"What's going to happen to her?" asked Solana.

"I don't know, honey," Teddy answered as they rejoined Katie and Dora. "That will be up to a judge to decide."

Solana nodded, and then she pointed to the workers who had gathered at the edge of the parade ground. "And what's going to happen to them?" The women were whispering in small groups, but making no effort to communicate with Teddy or Solana.

"I don't know. Do you, Katie?"

"No," she answered. "What happens here next is up to San Diego. We're just waiting for Maureen, and then we'll leave."

Teddy turned to Solana. "Solana, is there anything else you want to take with you? We won't be coming back. Is there anyone you want to say good-bye to?"

"Just my rabbit."

"You want to say good-bye to a rabbit? What rabbit?"

"No, to take him with me! He needs me to feed him."

Teddy gave Katie a stricken look.

Katie laughed. "Does he have a cage for riding in the car?"

"Yes, I think so," Solana said.

"Then go get him!"

A delighted Solana led Dora and Teddy back to the infirmary and showed them a makeshift wire enclosure where a white rabbit was sleeping.

Teddy was confounded. "Where did he come from?"

"I found him this morning. He was hiding, too."

"But I don't see a cage for him," said Teddy.

Dora laughed and said, "Don't worry!" She reached down for the rabbit and handed him to Teddy. "You carry the rabbit, and I'll rig up a cage for the ride home." She rolled up the length of chicken wire and put it under her arm. She then looked around the room and spotted a discarded piece of oilcloth.

"This will be the floor of his cage, in case he decides to go potty on the way home," she told Solana.

They went back to the car, where Dora wove the ends of the chicken wire together, making a cylindrical cage, which she put on the floor on the passenger's side. She laid the oilcloth down inside and molded it against the chicken wire; it came halfway up the sides of the "cage." She took the docile rabbit from Teddy and plopped him into his temporary home.

"There," Dora said to Solana. "He doesn't have much room, but it's only for two hours. When we get home, he can have a nice space in the chicken coop until I build him a house." She unwrapped her half-eaten sandwich and dropped a piece of it into the cage.

"You can build a house?" Solana asked admiringly.

"Sure! I'm a roofer!"

Teddy and Solana got into the backseat and started reading the books that Angela had found. Dora got into the driver's seat, and they waited, all doors but the rabbit's open to catch the breeze.

In the second car, Keisha was already interviewing Isabella, and Dawn was talking with Alicia.

Finally, Katie and Maureen came out of Big Mama's house. Teddy and Solana were absorbed with a picture book about a pet goat. Teddy's arm was around Solana, and Solana snuggled against him. At first, they didn't notice the new arrivals taking in the tableau.

"Hi, Maureen," said Teddy. "This is Solana!"

"Hello, pretty little girl," said Maureen.

Solana looked at Teddy for guidance. "She means you, Solana," he affirmed.

Solana smiled at Maureen, not quite as shy with a second Anglo woman. "I'm pleased to meet you."

"We're ready to leave now," Katie said. "Dora, will you please be the lead car again?"

Before heading to Maureen's car, Katie opened the front passenger-side door of her own car. "Very good-looking rabbit," she said to the backseat occupants. "Ingenious cage, Dora!"

After a brief word to Keisha, who was the driver of the second car, Maureen and Katie went to Maureen's car, and the three Los Angeles veggiemobiles headed for home.

Conversations on the Ride Home

Once she and Katie were out of earshot of the others, Maureen exploded with indignation. "That woman has been running a damn plantation!"

Katie agreed. "In the Old Days, the place would have been closed down for child endangerment, worker exploitation, and God knows what else."

"Did you see what she had inside her house?" Maureen asked. "She sure had a lot of nice things that she wasn't sharing with her workers."

"After seeing the woman's size," Katie said, "I just had to inspect the kitchen. There were lots of specialty items that I'll bet were never shared with the others—different kinds of candy, a freshly baked pie."

"She's a good candidate for diabetes," said Maureen. "She deserves that, and worse."

"I noticed," Katie said, "that Lauren seemed quite interested in some papers she'd found. I suspect that Big Mama will be charged with something bigger than her threat to us. Theft and fraud, maybe—after all, the place was supposed to be a cooperative."

Maureen, wanting to switch to another topic, said, "Well, it's really San Diego's problem and San Diego's decision."

"I always believed that San Diego had made a mistake," Katie mused, "leasing out large tracts of Pendleton in their rush to get the farmland productive again."

"I agree," said Maureen, "but was that really very different from our Council putting the clothing machines back into operation? If I remember, you were very much in favor of the Council going into the garment business."

Katie sighed. "I think it's very different. From what I could see, the profits at this farming commune weren't shared, and the workers had no say in its operation. In the case of the clothing factory, there was a big public demand to get the machines going again—some folks' clothes couldn't have withstood another patch! All of the garment workers share in the profits according to the number of hours they work, and there is a rotating management committee. The Council can suggest what products be made, based on suggestions from the Evaluation Cards, but the final decisions are made by the textile workers as a whole. I've been most impressed by the satisfaction people seem to get when they have control over their own work—even repetitive work like running a sewing machine. And look at the creativity that has exploded there! You're wearing one of my favorite examples right now—the kimono T-shirt. Before they started making these, how could you wear long sleeves and still keep cool?"

Maureen instinctively swung her right arm, creating a pleasant breeze within the garment. "Okay, Katie, I see what you mean. Maybe San Diego's goof was that they didn't screen this Ramona person, or ever check up on her operation. Did you see how filthy Solana's clothes are?"

"About as filthy as Teddy's were yesterday," Katie laughed. "Did you know that he came to the lecture barefooted?"

"I heard. It's good of you to take him and Solana in. Do you think that's going to work out?"

"There's been no time yet for a house meeting, but I think that will just be a formality, judging by the enthusiastic reception Teddy got last night." Katie spoke with conviction. "And the women are sure to love Solana after meeting her."

"She's adorable. I agree with you that Teddy should raise her—they definitely have quite a bond. So that's settled, then. I hope Keisha and Dawn make some progress with Alicia and Isabella."

They fell silent for a while and gazed out at the scenery. Long vistas of the Pacific Ocean swept by on their left.

Maureen then resumed the conversation. "The next thing we need to do is some records-crunching and find out Teddy's parentage. Big mystery there, since Big Mama claims she doesn't know Mary's family name. I guess we need to search the records for a 'Mary' who got inseminated nine months before Teddy's birth and for whom there is no further record."

Katie shook her head. "I don't think her name was Mary. She seems to have been running away from something. She may have been partly Asian—Isabella mentioned that there was something funny about her eyes; I think she was trying to describe an epicanthic fold, and there is a Japanese hotel sticker on one of Mary's suitcases."

"Oh, dear," said Maureen. This was beginning to look like a long, tedious task. "Would you be willing to do the record search, Katie?"

"Glad to. I'm feeling some urgency, as there's already an attraction beginning at the compound. The search will have to include at least a two-month period, since Teddy doesn't know his exact birthday. On the first of each month, the people at the commune had a birthday cake to celebrate all the birthdays that occurred in that month—so Teddy calls his birth date May 1, 2041."

Maureen was pleased to have delegated the task. "That means that the insemination could have occurred in August or September 2040. Good luck!"

She continued with a different piece of unfinished business. "Another thing, Katie. I only heard parts of your talk yesterday, but I caught the part where you asked to see the hands of women who knew they had donor sperm from your uncle Ralph. What was your thinking there? There's usually a hidden agenda behind your throw-away remarks."

Katie laughed at being found out by her old friend. "Two agendas, really. I think that women need to learn the identities of their sperm donors because many of them will be meeting their half brothers soon. Genetic counseling is all well and good, but we need to make our youth responsible themselves. Then there's the likelihood that we'll start having nuclear families again—mother, father, and child or children. I've been remembering a lot lately how dysfunctional my family was, as were so many other families I knew about when I was young. I hope that we're not going to foist the nuclear-family model onto a young couple that has an unplanned and unwanted pregnancy. Maybe a group of women who are all half sisters by virtue of having been fathered by the same donor—Ralph Kendall, for example—might do a better job in collectively raising a new Ralph K. baby. It's just a thought. It will either happen, or it won't!"

It was now Katie's turn to bring up a topic of concern. "Maureen, for the umpteenth time, you or someone *has* to make a public announcement that it's safe for men and boys to come out of hiding."

"Well, you certainly let the cat out of the bag yesterday!"

"It was only a shock for those who haven't heard the rumors or spotted a man out somewhere," Katie said. "Dora said she even saw a guy with a full beard. Now *that's* making a statement!"

"Or having no access to a razor."

Katie allowed herself to be distracted for a moment. "Yes, I had to search quite a bit before I found one of Dad's old razors for Teddy. It was rather like the Old Days to watch a man shave." She drifted into a reverie in which she compared Peter with Teddy. She looked out the window; they were well into Los Angeles County and would be home soon.

Unwilling to let Maureen stay off topic, Katie challenged her: "Maureen, you haven't answered me. When are you going to make that announcement?"

Maureen responded primly, as if quoting another person. "The Council wants to make sure it's completely safe and wants to put the question on the Evaluation Form in November."

This angered Katie. "Maureen, the men and boys are voting already—with their feet! What's unsafe is all the second-generation *unregistered* births we'll be having— the wrong people mating with one another and, incidentally, screwing up our data."

Maureen had heard this argument quite a few times already. She turned to look squarely at Katie. "Sometimes," she said testily, "I think you care more about your damned data than the people involved."

Katie reached out with her left hand, as if to take over the steering. "Please keep your eyes on the damn road. You know that's not true. I care about those guys cooped up in apartments, wasting their lives." She calmed down a bit and added, "And yes, if it turns out that any of the men are susceptible to the GSV, I want to know as soon as possible which kind of amended-Y was used in their conception, so that we can stop using that variety."

Maureen, now carefully keeping her eyes on the road, reached out to touch her friend's arm. "I'm sorry, Katie. No one cares more about people than you. I wish you hadn't resigned all your posts. It's hard to bear the torch without you. But I'm up against those conservative factions on both the Council and the Genetics Committee that want to maintain the status quo. They're so fearful of making a mistake! They don't want to be accused of 'playing God.' You know, you really stirred up something yesterday with your innocent little birthday speech."

Katie giggled like the impish child she once was. "Maureen, that was why I resigned! So I would feel free to make that speech!"

Maureen let out a sigh. "I should have guessed."

They both fell quiet again.

When Katie resumed talking, it was in a different mode. "I know something about playing God, Maureen. I didn't do a full confessional yesterday. *We* were playing God when we decided who could be inseminated, and with whose sperm. When I was reciting what I missed about the Old Days, I didn't mention the loss of diversity in our species—all the different ethnic backgrounds, the different colors of skin and hair. No more redheads like you, Maureen! I still believe that it was a good decision to inseminate minority women with Anglo sperm, but there's a downside. With everybody being *'café-au-lait,'* as I was bragging, I find them damn boring to look at sometimes. Don't you?"

Maureen was charmed by Katie's confession. "Yes and no," she said. "I like being one of the rare redheads. But there's another downside that maybe hasn't occurred to you, being older. When I turned fifty and liked to think that I really only looked thirty, I couldn't pass for thirty, because I wasn't your '*café au lait.*'"

"Maureen, I never guessed that you were vain!" Katie seemed delighted.

"We all are, Katie, if you look hard enough."

"You're right." The two women had regained their customary level of affection and mutual appreciation.

They were distracted by a toot from Keisha's car and a good-bye wave out the window from Dawn as that car turned onto a side-road. "Where they are going?" Katie asked.

"Possibly to Keisha's for the night," answered Maureen. "I told them to use their own judgment about where to take Alicia and Isabella. I'll hear from them tomorrow, after the women have had their medical checkup."

*   *   *   *

In the lead car, Dora announced, "We're almost there!"

"There's something I want to ask you," Teddy said hurriedly. "Do you have a cooking buddy?"

"Yes. Carolyn."

"Oh." Teddy's voice betrayed his disappointment.

"Why do you ask?"

"Katie told me this morning about the dinner rotation. I really don't know much about cooking, so I was hoping to buddy up with someone. That was such a good meal you fixed last night! I'd like to learn how to cook like that."

"I'd love to have you buddy with me, actually." Dora was genuinely enthusiastic. "Carolyn means well, but she so often has to stay late at the hospital that I cook alone on both of our nights most of the time. With three nights in the rotation schedule, you'd have a crash course in Dora-style cuisine."

"Thanks," Teddy answered, relieved. "That would be wonderful!"

Solana seemed perplexed, and Teddy explained, "Your daddy is going to learn to be a good cook, like Dora."

"Could I help too, Dora?" Solana asked.

Dora grinned at Solana in the rear-view mirror and said, "You're on! I'll bet you're an expert pea sheller!"

Biology House, 5 PM

The two veggiemobiles containing Katie, Maureen, Dora, Teddy, and Solana arrived at Biology House, where they found multicolored balloons tied to bushes and trees and a huge "Welcome, Solana" sign on the front door. Solana was entranced. She ran up to each balloon and touched it. Dora and Teddy harvested a few and handed them to her. Solana paused at the door and pointed at the sign. "That's my name!" she said.

"Do you know what the first word says?" Katie asked her.

Solana shook her head. "It says 'Welcome,'" Katie said. "Welcome to your new home!"

Inside, many women applauded upon seeing Solana, then came forward to tell her their names. Solana looked a bit overwhelmed and clung tightly to Teddy's hand. Chris came forward and asked Solana about the rabbit Dora carried. "Is this your rabbit?" Solana nodded. "I'm very fond of rabbits, too. What's his name?"

"Bunny."

"Why don't we go find a nice cool place outdoors for him?" Chris suggested. "And get him some water, and something to eat. What does he like to eat?"

"Lettuce, carrots ... anything left over." Chris, Dora, and Solana left through the kitchen.

Virginia approached Maureen and Katie. "Hello, Maureen. I hope you can stay for supper. We're having a barbecue—chicken and veggie-dogs." She turned to Katie and said, "The whole compound is coming. History House is bringing the salad, and Third House has a surprise dessert. We've also invited that couple on the next block and their six-year-old daughter. They've given Solana lots of Roweena's hand-me-downs and a mattress that Ro has outgrown."

"That sounds great!" said Katie. "You women have been busy. I'm so glad someone thought about Roweena."

"That was Angela's idea," Virginia said.

"What time is supper?" Katie asked. "That child needs a bath before she meets any more people!"

"It's not supper until I ring the bell. And people have been asked not to swarm Teddy and Solana."

*   *   *   *

Katie and Maureen went to inspect Bunny's new habitat in the shade of an avocado tree. Dora had used the length of chicken wire purloined from Pendleton to enclose a corner of the chicken run. The rabbit happily chewed on some lettuce. "Would you like to pet him?" Solana asked.

Katie and Maureen each stroked the rabbit's ears. "Solana," Katie said, "would you like a nice tub-bath before dinner?"

"Can my daddy come, too?"

"Of course."

*   *   *   *

On the way to Katie's bathroom, Chris, Teddy, and Solana passed by Teddy's bedroom. Indicating the child-sized mattress on the floor, Chris said, "This is your daddy's room, and this will be your bed until you get bigger." Solana ran to the mattress and picked up the teddy bear that had been sitting propped up by the pillow. "That's a present from Roweena, a little girl you'll meet at supper."

"Is she my age?"

"A few years older—she's already in school. But she's not much taller than you."

Chris combed the tangles out of Solana's hair before helping her into the bathtub. She gave Solana a shampoo while Teddy helped Solana bathe the rest of herself. After Chris left the room to get a towel, Solana asked Teddy, "Which lady are you going to sleep with tonight?"

Teddy was rather startled by this question. "No one, honey, no one."

"Won't Katie make you?"

"No, no. She's nothing like Big Mama. This is a very different place. You'll see." Teddy realized that Katie and Chris might have overheard the conversation, and he felt embarrassed.

Katie appeared soon afterward, holding up a party dress in one hand and a T-shirt and jeans in the other. "Would you like to wear either of these tonight? They were Roweena's."

"The dress! The dress!" Solana was ecstatic. "It looks like in the movies!"

After Solana was dried off, the group moved into Katie's bedroom. Solana immediately spotted a very large plush dog on Katie's bed.

"What a big bear!" she exclaimed.

"Actually, it's a dog, not a bear," said Katie.

"I've seen dogs in the movies," Solana volunteered. "Why do you have a dog on your bed? Do you sleep with him?"

Katie nodded. "I sure do. I found him in an abandoned house. He looked so much like the dog that I lost in the Great Disaster that I just had to bring him home."

"What's his name?"

"Paul Revere."

Solana stroked Paul Revere as Katie helped her on with her new dress, panties, and sandals. "You know, Solana," Katie said, "I never had any children, so of course I never got to be a grandmother. I was wondering if you would let me be a pretend-grandmother to you."

"I've never had a grandmother. What do grandmothers do?"

"Well, they take care of their grandchildren when their parents are at work or at the University. They spoil the grandchildren, hug them a lot, give them treats, tell them stories … At least, that's how it was with me and my grandmother Lisa."

"I think I'd like to have a grandmother. What shall I call you?"

"Katie, or Grandmother, or whatever you like!"

"I think I'll call you Grandmother Katie." Solana allowed Katie to hug her, and then she hopped off the bed. When she saw herself in a full-length mirror, she was transformed. She pirouetted and curtsied to her image.

"Are you ready to go meet some more people and have a barbecue?" Katie asked.

"Sure!" replied the now-confident Solana. Holding hands with Katie and Teddy, Solana descended into the backyard. Many people had gathered there, all of them wearing tags with their first names. Solana released her two escorts and went into the crowd, introducing herself to each person individually. "Hello, I'm Solana. What's your name?"

An astonished Katie watched this performance. "Wherever did she learn to behave like this?" she asked Teddy.

"From the movies," Teddy said proudly. "There was one film in which a little girl played hostess just like this, in a very rich person's house. The next morning, Solana greeted everyone this way, but only a few people played along with her. I think she's following the same script now."

Solana met a young woman named Ashley. She pointed to Ashley's name tag and said, "A is for apple."

Soon, Solana had found Roweena. "Thank you for this dress. I just love it! Do you want to see my rabbit?" The two girls disappeared in the direction of the makeshift hutch.

Virginia, who had also been observing the performance, joined Teddy and Katie. "What a happy child! Teddy, you've done such a great job of raising her despite what I hear was a most miserable environment."

"Did you notice her interest in the name-tags?" Katie asked Virginia. "She seems to know her ABCs. Is she ready for preschool, do you think?"

"Definitely. And she's going to read early. But for the first week, I'd keep her with you or Teddy. Before long, I'm sure she'll ask to go to school!"

Katie turned to Teddy and said, "Tomorrow, I'm going to be spending most of the day at the computer in the records room, chasing down your genealogy. Solana could come with me, along with some books and coloring books, and you could drop in on us between classes."

"That sounds like a good plan," Teddy answered. "Have you seen Angela?"

The three of them drifted apart. Teddy was pretty obviously searching the crowd for Angela, but also responding politely to anyone who stopped him with comments.

Teddy found Angela in the kitchen of History House, preparing a salad. "I found you!" He gave her a brief hug. "Are you coming to the barbecue? I want you to meet Solana."

"I'm dying to meet her, but it's my night to cook. I need to finish up this second load of salad."

Teddy washed his hands and started chopping up the carrots that were lying on the drain-board. "Those are great clothes that you found for Solana. She's never had a dress before, and she loves wearing it."

"Were there any problems at the commune?" Angela asked.

"Big Mama started to object, but then someone from the San Diego Council made a very legal sort of speech, and I heard Big Mama's name for the first time— Ramona Morales. Big Mama tried to pick a fight and told Lupe to go get their gun, and she ended up being arrested."

"That's a relief! Was Solana's mother upset to have Solana taken away?"

"Not a bit," Teddy snorted. "She didn't even say good-bye, and Solana didn't want to say good-bye to her or anyone else. I think she's as relieved as I am to be away from that place."

Chris and Solana came into the kitchen. "Someone wanted to know where her daddy was," Chris said, "and I figured that we'd find you here." Solana grabbed Teddy's hand.

He picked her up and said, "Solana, this is Angela."

Solana extended her hand and said, "Hello, Angela, I'm very pleased to meet you." Her formality then vanished, and she said, "I just love this dress! Thank you!" Solana jumped down and twirled around.

"You're very welcome. I'm so glad that you're going to live here!" Angela hugged the child.

"This is enough salad for seven communes," Chris said. "Let's go." They picked up the tubs of salad and went next door.

Soon after arriving at the barbecue, Angela found Katie standing alone. Angela gave her a big hug and whispered, "Hello, Cousin Katie!"

Katie grinned. "I do love it when people take my advice! I thought you might like to know that Cameron wasn't the only Kendall in History House!"

It was a happy party, with people eating, talking, laughing, and joking. Roweena and Solana played "You Can't Catch Me" with several of the younger women and Teddy. When Teddy would catch Solana, he would pick her up and hold her high in the air.

Roweena watched this happen a few times. Then she deliberately placed herself in front of Teddy, clearly wanting the same treatment. Without missing a beat, he picked her up and swung her back and forth. Roweena shrieked with delight. Then it was Solana's turn again. After a while, Dora intercepted the girls to give Teddy a break.

The party ended when Roweena's mothers decided that it was her bedtime. "It's a school day tomorrow, so we should go," Margaret said to Teddy. "Our girls had such a good time together, didn't they? We'd like you to come over for supper as soon as you feel settled."

Teddy found Angela. "It's Solana's bedtime, too," he said. "She's had a pretty exciting day. I'll be going to bed at the same time, to make her feel secure. So this is good night, then." He stroked her arm. "Will I see you tomorrow?"

"Maybe lunch in the cafeteria?" Angela suggested.

Teddy took Solana by the hand and got the attention of the crowd. "Good night, everyone! I want to thank you all again for the wonderful welcome you've given to Solana and me. I'll try to be worthy of your friendship."

"Good night, everyone!" Solana chimed in. "Thank you for the nice party."

The group applauded and blew kisses as father and daughter left the party and entered the house.

*   *   *   *

Teddy kissed Solana good-night and climbed into his own bed.

A few minutes later, a small voice piped up. "Daddy?"

"Yes?"

"Is Angela the lady that you like the best?"

"Honey, I like them all. Angela was the first one I met, and she helped me to meet Katie, so we owe her a lot."

"Uh-huh. And she asked Roweena for clothes for me."

"Yes, she likes you a lot."

Solana was dubious. "But she got me the clothes before she met me."

"Well, I told her a lot about you, so she knew that she would love you. Time to go to sleep!"

After Teddy fell asleep, Solana got up, looked out the window in the direction of the avocado tree and her rabbit, and then glanced down the hill to History House. Still holding her teddy bear, she crept into Teddy's bed. Half awake, he moved over and put an arm around her, and they fell asleep, spoon-fashion.

*   *   *   *

Down in the yard, Angela, Katie, and Chris were finishing the cleanup after the night's festivities. "What's Teddy's schedule tomorrow?" Angela asked Katie. "He asked me if we could have lunch together."

"I'm not sure. He's going to check in on me and Solana in the records room between classes. Let's try for lunch in the cafeteria at noon." Katie's sweeping gesture included Chris in the invitation.

"Okay," said Angela. "See you there. 'Night!" She left to go to History House.

Chris looked after her wistfully. "What's the matter, Chris?" Katie asked. "You look sad."

"It's too late for me, Katie. I was born too soon."

"Too soon for …?"

"All these young men who are going to be surviving and joining our society … they're all going to be Teddy's age and younger. I'm twenty-eight."

"Hm, yes. that *is* a bit of a discrepancy. So, you find Teddy attractive?"

"I'm afraid so. But he's already found the woman he wants." Chris sighed. "Are all the men going to be this good-looking and, well …"

"Sexy? Some yes, some no. Teddy has a special charisma, partly because he's just such a nice person. He reminds me so much of Peter … Most of the women Peter met were turned on to him, and he was mostly oblivious to it. I think that a lot of the women's heads were turned by Teddy tonight."

"I thought so, too. Well … good night, Katie."

"Sleep well, Chris. Find us for lunch tomorrow." Katie started toward the back door of the house, then paused and turned back to face Chris. "Incidentally, in the Old Days, some men preferred older women." With an impish grin, she was gone before Chris could respond.

*   *   *   *

Very tired, Katie climbed into bed, wrapped herself around Paul Revere, and, as was her nightly custom, spoke to Peter in a soft whisper. "Isn't your granddaughter an absolutely delightful child? And aren't you proud of what a good father Teddy is? Just like you would have been. I thought that I might be joining you soon, now that my work with the Y chromosome is finished. But I'm sorry … it's going to have to be a while yet. I need to stay on a while longer to see that Solana and Teddy are all right. How I wish you could have been here today!" She drifted off to sleep with a contented smile on her face.

Thursday, August 19

Maureen poked her head into the records room. Katie was busy at the computer, and Solana was drawing with colored pencils.

"Hi, Katie. I thought I'd look in to see how you were doing. Good morning, Solana."

"Hello, Grandmother Maureen. Would you like a picture?" Solana handed Maureen a colorful drawing of what might have been a rabbit ... or perhaps a house. In any case, there was definitely green grass in the foreground.

"Well, thank you, dear," said Maureen. She hugged the child, who then went back to her coloring.

"Katie, I think I've just been promoted!" Maureen seemed delighted.

"I don't think she feels comfortable calling us older folks by our first names," Katie explained. "It's probably something else she picked up from the movies! I was about to call you. I think I've found Teddy's birth mother. If I'm right, her name was Machiko Takahashi."

"So soon? You must have had to go through several thousand records."

"Not really. I looked at only the inseminations involving amended Y chromosomes, since they produced the only children who would have survived to Teddy's age. And then I narrowed the search to semen from Peter V. There's only one insemination using his sperm where there is no record of either birth or miscarriage, and that was Machiko's."

"Peter V! You mean Peter, your old boyfriend? How do you know?"

"Maureen, Teddy looks and walks so much like Peter. I had him pegged before he reached the stage at my lecture."

"And you never said a word."

"No, I guess I was afraid …"

"That the Genetics Committee would step in and take Teddy away from you?" Maureen pulled a chair close to Katie, took her hands, and held one of them to her own cheek. "Oh, Katie! No fear, times have changed." Katie visibly relaxed.

"Of course, I wasn't on the Committee at the time of the Great Disaster," Maureen continued, "but I heard later about Carmen asking Maria to let you have a child by Peter, and about Maria's curt refusal. The Committee talked about it quite a number of years later, and everyone serving at that time agreed that we would have honored the request. In a way, that semen was yours. You had brought it from Boston; you kept it safe throughout South America …"

"Carmen asked Maria? I never knew! She never told me. That sweet, unselfish woman!" Katie was stunned.

They were interrupted by the Teddy's arrival and the eruption of Solana into his arms. He sat down and held Solana on his lap while she showed him her latest pictures.

"So, how was the advanced calculus class?" Katie asked.

"Not easy. That calculus book I read must have been pretty elementary. I'm going to have to work really hard to catch up to the class."

"You wouldn't rather drop the advanced class and take the beginner class?" Maureen asked.

"No, I don't think so. It wouldn't be a challenge. And I like this professor a lot." Solana, bored with this grown-up conversation, jumped off his lap and went back to her coloring.

Katie took advantage of Solana's departure. "I have good news, Teddy. I think that I've discovered your parents' identities. But first, I'd like to show you some photos. Tell me if you recognize any of these women."

Katie went to a table and, one at a time, laid down pictures of women that had been taken at the time of their inseminations. Teddy shook his head quickly at the first one.

He picked up the second picture, studied it a bit, and then said, "I'm not sure, but is this Margaret? One of Roweena's mothers?"

"Right on." Katie put down the third one, and Teddy shook his head.

Upon seeing the fourth picture, Teddy shouted, "That's Mary! That's my mother! She looks so young and pretty here. When was this taken?"

"When she was inseminated. Her name is Machiko Takahashi. She was an artist and a student at the U. And this is a picture of Machiko's mother, a Japanese American with Japanese ancestry on both sides. Her name is Takara Takahashi, and, if she is still living, she would be sixty-five now."

Teddy was ecstatic. "Oh, my goodness! Solana, this is a picture of your grand-mother."

Solana solemnly examined the picture of a pretty young Japanese girl and pro-claimed, "She looks too young to be a grandmother."

"That's because this picture was taken before *I* was born," Teddy explained, "much less you."

"Did you find out who my father was?" he asked Katie.

"Yes. His name was Peter Vlatas. He was a computer engineer of Greek ancestry on both sides."

"Do you have his picture?"

"No, I'm afraid not. But if you want to know what he looked like, just look in the mirror."

"Katie, you mean ... *your* Peter?" Teddy was incredulous.

"Absolutely." Katie's voice cracked just a little.

Teddy embraced her, almost crying. "Katie, I feel so honored."

"Peter would be so very proud of you. I want you to know that. Always remember it."

Chris pushed the door all the way open and surveyed the room. "Hello, every-body! Who's ready for lunch?"

An exuberant Teddy told her, "Katie found my parents! And my father was Peter Vlatas ... *her* Peter!"

"Wow! That's amazing!"

"And this is a picture of my mother," Teddy continued. "Her name was Machiko, not Mary. She was half Japanese."

Chris looked at the picture. "She's beautiful. But such a tiny person! You must have gotten your height genes from this Peter ... What was his name? Oh, my God, not Peter V?"

"Yes, Peter V," Katie said. "V for Vlatas." She was enjoying this dramatic moment immensely.

Chris shrieked with delight. "Teddy, you're my brother! I'm your sister! I just came from the registry!"

"Sister!" Teddy hugged her, and they danced around together. Chris pulled Katie in for a group hug. Solana wasn't willing to be left out and wormed her way into the circle.

Angela arrived in time to witness this display of affection and stood in the door-way feeling tense and uncomfortable. She watched as Teddy explained to Solana.

"Solana, Chris is your aunt!"

"That's nice," said Solana, unimpressed.

"Chris and I have the same father, so we're brother and sister. His name was Peter Vlatas, and Katie knew him a long time ago."

Teddy looked up as Angela entered the room. "You heard the news?"

Relieved, Angela answered, "Yes, that's fantastic! Let me look at the two of you together." She took Chris's hand and positioned her beside Teddy. "There really *is* a resemblance. You're both tall, and you both have the same merry eyes. What do you think, Solana? Do they look like brother and sister?"

This was all very confusing to Solana, who answered, "I'm not sure what brothers and sisters are."

"When a mother and a father have both a boy child and a girl child," Teddy explained, "the two children are called brother and sister. Don't you remember about brothers and sisters from the movies?"

"But there *aren't* any little boys any more," said the puzzled child.

Chris nodded gleefully. "Oh, I think there are! I think you'll be meeting some little boys before too long."

"You mean, I might have a brother?" Solana was becoming quite interested.

Chris looked at the others in the room and stifled a giggle. "Yes, I'm pretty sure you do."

"I think I'd like to have a brother. And maybe a sister, too."

Katie looked at her watch. "Why don't you four go on to the cafeteria? I need to talk to Maureen about a few things. Get a big table, and we'll join you shortly."

"All right." Teddy took Solana by the hand, and they all started to leave.

In the doorway, Chris turned and asked Katie, "You already knew about me and Peter V, didn't you?" Katie nodded. "For how long?"

"I'll tell you later."

"All right. I just want to tell you that I'm very happy to be a Peter V product. It makes me feel related to you!"

Katie blew her a kiss, then closed the door after her.

"Okay, Katie, what now?" Maureen was half afraid of a repeat of the previous day's conversation.

"I think we need to do a sort for Peter V inseminations and identify all of Teddy's half-sisters."

"What then? Send them all a letter warning them not to fornicate with him?" Maureen wasn't as concerned as Katie with the consanguinity problem, and she sometimes found Katie to be a bit obsessive about the subject.

Katie giggled. "That would be one way! I was just thinking to give Teddy a list of his half sisters. He's a very responsible person."

"Or we could throw a big party for all of Peter V's descendants!"

"You're making fun of me again," Katie said. "Actually, that's not a bad idea—unless the list is too large. Peter *was* one of our major donors."

"Indeed he was."

"I have your permission to do the sort, then?"

"Of course you do, Katie. You don't have to ask!"

"But I resigned …"

"And I never accepted your resignation, Katie. Go ahead, have fun!"

"Thanks, Maureen. And just one more thing …"

Maureen groaned. "My stomach is rumbling. What now?"

"I think that the registry should start including the last names of the sperm donors. Peter Vlatas instead of just Peter V, for instance. And it should include the brief descriptions we have of the donors—height, age, hair and eye color, ancestry, and so on. And pictures, if we have them. The women won't be satisfied with just a name, and we'll be getting a lot of inquiries. Better to have all this information readily available."

Maureen was enthusiastic. "Of course! Definitely, we need to do that. I'll put some people to work on it right away. Now, lunch?"

*   *   *   *

On their walk to the cafeteria many women noticed Teddy, and some made comments to their companions. Some women called out, "Hi, Teddy!" as they passed by.

Solana, taking this all in, asked, "Why is everybody looking at you, Daddy?"

"Good question!" said Angela. "I've never felt quite so conspicuous!"

"It's worse when I don't have you three with me for protection," Teddy said. To Solana, he said, "I think they're just curious, honey. Some of them might never have seen a man—someone who is a daddy—before."

"Oh, okay," said Solana. But she continued to observe the interested women.

"I can hardly wait for some other men to come out," said Teddy, "and take the spotlight off me. I had two very attractive young women offer to tutor me in calculus today. I sure could use some tutoring, but I don't think that was all they were offering."

"You're turning them on, Brother!" Chris said.

"That's all very nice, but I've already met the woman I want in my life." Teddy put his arm around Angela's shoulders and gave her a quick kiss on the forehead.

Angela was very pleased with the public acknowledgment, but felt uncomfortable at the same time.

*   *   *   *

Late that afternoon, Chris searched through all the common areas of Biology House for Katie and finally found her out in the backyard, sitting on a bench and watching Solana play with her rabbit.

"The rabbit has been given a real name," said Katie as Chris joined her on the bench. "It's George."

"He's so docile; I wonder if he was somebody's house rabbit?"

"I've been wondering the same thing! But let's not give anybody any ideas."

"Agreed," said Chris. "Katie, you were going to tell me …"

"Oh yes. Do you remember when you came to fix that first computer … gosh, how many years ago?"

"I think about nine. And I was delighted—and very surprised—that you suggested renovating the old garage into a computer shop for me."

"Well, I liked you immediately, and I admired how clever and intuitive you were at such a young age. I was concerned about your finding a new place to live—you remember that you were getting restless living in that apartment with your two mothers, and I quite selfishly realized how nice it would be to have a resident computer guru. And so, I made my invitation. Then, that very night, I had a dream that made me realize how much you resembled Peter, which I hadn't consciously noticed. The next day, using my special prerogatives, I went and looked you up. And, sure enough, you were Peter's daughter!"

"But you never told me!"

"And confess that I'd broken a rule and invaded your privacy?" Katie laughed.

"It felt better not to. And you didn't need to have a third mother! But you've always been an almost-daughter in my heart."

"I think all of us at Biology House feel mothered by you—but it's the unobtrusive kind of mothering." Chris gave Katie a hug and a kiss. "Got to go; my night to cook."

*   *   *   *

Someone else had some unfinished business to take care of that evening. After Teddy had put Solana to bed, he gathered up his textbooks and went next door to History House.

Angela was busily typing at a computer. She looked up at Teddy and gave him a welcoming smile. "Hi. Give me five or ten minutes to finish this little bit. You know

Martha." She indicated the woman at the next monitor. "And Mercedes and Beth." She pointed to the two women sprawled in some armchairs by the window.

"Sure thing," said Teddy. "I brought my calculus homework." He settled himself into the couch near Beth and Mercedes.

"How's school?" Mercedes asked. "What classes are you taking?"

"I'm trying out calculus, physics, and history, so far."

"History! Which class?" Both women seemed interested.

"It's called 'The United States from its Early Beginnings,'" answered Teddy. The two women looked at one another and groaned.

"I don't like it either," said Teddy. "I don't think I'm going back." He reconsidered. "Well, I'll have to go back once. To return the textbook."

"The quarter's nearly over," Beth said, "but I'll bet she's still going on about all the battles of the French and Indian War."

"You're right! So far, no American Revolution! So tell me, what's a good course on the United States in the twentieth century?"

Mercedes answered, looking fondly toward Angela, "Well, until Angela finishes her dissertation and starts teaching herself, your best bet would be any of Dr. Porter's classes. And maybe you don't know that we have a great collection of history books here." She swept a hand around at all the bookcases in the room. "Everyone in the compound has borrowing privileges."

With that, Angela closed her file and turned off the computer. She patted Mercedes on the shoulder, said "Thanks for the PR!" and joined Teddy on the couch.

"Well, how was the physics, then?" she asked.

"Really easy." Teddy sounded relieved. "I knew a lot of it already, but I won't drop the course. I like the professor, and I really need to have a firm foundation in physics."

Martha turned off her computer and spoke to the group. "I'm headed for bed. But first, I wondered if you'd like to hear the gossip about Cameron and Brandy."

"Of course!" yelled Beth.

"Does a cat like to lick its fur?" said Mercedes.

"This will be all over the campus tomorrow," Martha said, "but don't tell anyone I was your source, and *please* act surprised when someone tells you about it. I'd rather not have it look as though the information came from History House."

"Mum's the word," Mercedes promised, and the others nodded.

"Brandy and Cameron failed their evaluation today!"

There was "Hooray!" from Beth and a "Justice is served!" from Mercedes. They high-fived one another.

Angela reacted more soberly. "Do you know why?" she asked.

"The Committee thought that the relationship was too new, that it had begun under questionable circumstances, and that Cameron is too controlling," Martha said. "Now this next bit is *very* confidential: Parker told me that Cameron is *never* going to get a child with *any* partner."

"Now I'm off to bed, really." Martha headed for the stairs. "Me, too," said Mercedes and Beth almost simultaneously. Soon, Teddy and Angela were alone in the living room.

"Do you feel bad that Cameron has been ... what, permanently disqualified?" Teddy asked. Angela had made no rejoicing sounds upon hearing the news.

"No, I don't," she said. "I don't know why I didn't see it before, but Cameron would be an absolutely terrible mother. And I feel somewhat horrified that I ever considered it even for a minute—asking for insemination with her as co-mother."

"Do you feel that you and Cameron are finished? That's really what I came to ask you."

"Definitely finished. But I need to do some writing in my diary before I understand how I came to get involved in what was really an abusive relationship. No physical abuse—just allowing her to dominate me so."

"I'm relieved that you feel finished with her," said Teddy. "I also want to know if I was out of line when I kissed you on our way to lunch today. I see women kissing and hugging each other on campus, and there sure is a lot of hugging in the compound ..."

Angela leaned over and kissed him on the cheek. "That was quite all right. I liked it. We're an affectionate bunch of people—pretty different from that commune you escaped from."

Teddy reached for her hand and held it. "But I don't feel affectionate with just everyone. You're very special to me. I think I fell in love with you in Room 232."

"Teddy, this is Day Three. I've only known you for three days. And I'm the first woman your age that you've ever spoken to!"

"That's true. But that has nothing to do with what I feel for you.. Don't you feel anything for me?"

"Teddy, I care for you a lot. I look forward to seeing you. I feel really comfortable with you ... like we can talk about anything together. I love your sensitivity to other people and marvel at how you managed to develop it. I think that you're a wonderful father. But it's too soon to call it 'love.'"

Teddy hugged her and kissed her forehead, "I'll settle for that, for now."

In unspoken agreement, they opened their books to study and snuggled against one another as they read.

After a half-hour, Teddy turned to Angela and said, "Something's bothering me. How did Martha know all that about Cameron and Brandy? And so soon?"

Angela put her book down. "Martha told us at dinner last night that the Genetics Committee had asked her to come and see them today. So she asked us—and particularly me—if there was anything that we wanted withheld. We said, 'No! Tell them everything!'" Angela looked at him. "You seem bothered by this."

"I just thought that there was more respect for people's privacy here. I was used to the lack of it at the commune, but I thought that things were different here."

"Oh, they are; basically, we do respect one another's privacy. For instance, if someone's door is closed, you knock, and if no one answers, you leave. But nothing's really private any more if you want to be evaluated for insemination. The reasoning is that sperm is so precious, and a good emotional environment is just as important for a child as a biologically healthy young mother. Therefore, it's okay for the Committee to be very, very nosy. By and large, they do a good job with their evaluations. Most of the children I know have very stable, happy homes—like Roweena, for instance." Teddy nodded.

"The Committee must have had an off day when they evaluated Patsy and Cindy, however," Angela added with a rueful laugh.

"I think I understand now," Teddy said. "Thanks." He stood up and said, "I think it's my bedtime."

"Mine too," Said Angela. She stood as well, and presented herself for a good-night hug. Teddy wrapped her in his arms and stroked her hair. They separated, their eyes met, and Teddy kissed her tenderly on the lips.

Angela looked up at him. Before she realized quite what she was doing, she put both hands on his face and, standing on her tiptoes, pulled his face toward her and kissed him with a passion that surprised them both. "Bye," she whispered, and she ran toward the stairs.

A very happy Teddy left History House and headed for home.

Friday, August 20

Chris, Teddy, and Solana had just finished breakfast. Teddy was washing their dishes, and Chris was drying them. Teddy stooped down and kissed Solana. "Bye, honey, I'm off to school!" he said.

"Daddy, I want to go too." Solana said.

"Can't do," Teddy answered calmly.

"You can watch me work," Chris said. "Or color. Katie will be up pretty soon, and Dora's going to build that hutch for George this afternoon. Didn't you want to help her?"

Teddy mounted the bike that Katie had said could be his, and was soon happy to be alone with his thoughts. He enjoyed the slower journey to the U, during which he was able to take in more details. There were lots of other bicyclists headed the same direction, as well as a few scooters. Many people waved to him, and he waved back, relieved that he could be friendly without having to talk to all these women.

He noticed the wide variety of scooters. There was the standard one-seater type, just like in the movies. Another kind had a second seat just behind the driver, and the passenger had to hold tight to the driver to keep from falling off. *That looks pretty cozy*, he thought, imagining himself driving with Angela's arms tight around his waist.

A scooter passed him that had a sidecar attached. One woman was driving; the other woman in the sidecar was reading a book, paying no attention to either driver or scenery. *She must be used to both,* thought Teddy. There were two book bags at her feet.

He was particularly intrigued with what looked like individual innovations. One scooter pulled a long, boxy structure—whatever was within the extension was concealed and contained by a tarp that seemed to be firmly attached by some cords. One scooter that caused Teddy to chuckle had a sidecar and a canopy that covered both driver and passenger. *Great for a hot, sunny day,* he thought. *Not too great for windy weather.*

He found a bike slot near the Math Building and slid his bike in. As he walked toward the building, a tall woman emerged from behind a bush. *Oh, dear, another one,* thought Teddy.

"Teddy, I need to talk to you."

This wasn't a woman's voice! "Wow! I need to talk to you, too!" Teddy turned to face the young man, a little shorter than he, with a just-beginning beard. He held out his hand.

The young man grasped it vigorously and led Teddy behind the bush. "I saw you here yesterday, and I thought you might be back, so I waited here for you." He let go of Teddy's hand.

"Not overnight, I hope," Teddy said.

"No, no. I went back home before my mothers came home from work. I've been sneaking out almost every day for more than a month, exploring and hoping to meet another man. My name's Billy."

"Billy, I can't tell you how glad I am to meet *you*," Teddy exclaimed. He held out his hand again, and after an exchange of looks, the two men fell into a hug. Then they separated, each looking the other over appraisingly.

"How did you know my name?" Teddy asked.

"Everybody knows who you are! I hear a lot of the women talking about you. And I snuck into Katie Kendall's lecture on Tuesday. I was hiding at the back of the auditorium, but I got there only after Katie had taken you away."

"I've got a class that's starting in a minute, but we've got to talk more! Can you meet me for lunch in the cafeteria?"

Billy looked panic-stricken at the suggestion, so Teddy amended his idea. "I'll meet you here after class, in about an hour. We can walk to the cafeteria together. How's that?"

Billy nodded, but he still looked nervous.

"What do you need to talk to me about so badly?" asked Teddy.

"Just—is it really safe to be out? How did you get into the U? What is it like?"

"Yes, it's safe. Really, really safe. You don't have to be afraid of anything except being swarmed by all these curious college women." Teddy slapped Billy reassuringly on the shoulder. "I'll tell you the rest at lunch." With that, he dashed into the building. Billy retreated further behind his bush and took a book out of his backpack.

*   *   *   *

An hour later, the sound of many footsteps alerted Billy to the change of classes. He waited, but Teddy didn't appear. *He's forgotten about me,* thought the tremendously disappointed young man. Then he heard voices and peeked out. It was Teddy and two women.

"Hey, thanks a lot, but I'm meeting someone for lunch," said Teddy, kindly but firmly.

'We're headed that way, so we can go with you," one of the women proposed.

"Not headed that way yet. See you Monday!" Teddy went back into the building. Billy waited a few minutes longer, and then Teddy slipped into his hiding-place.

"I'm sorry it took me so long. I had to shake off two women," Teddy apologized.

"I heard, and I saw. They were both pretty!"

"If you want a girlfriend, you'll have a lot to choose from," said Teddy. "When you meet them individually, in some normal way, they're all very nice. I just find the unbridled curiosity of strangers a little unnerving."

"Two weeks ago, a woman spotted me, realized I was a man, and, when I didn't want to talk to her and ran away, she chased me. But I could run faster!"

"As soon as there are more of us out there, it will be different," Teddy said. "Now, let's get ready to walk the gauntlet. The best way to do it is to keep looking at one another, keep talking about something interesting, and not look at any of the women."

They left the safety of the bush, and Teddy started the conversation. "What are you doing about the beard problem? It's pretty hard to look like a woman with stubble on the chin!"

"Tell me about it! I've asked my mothers for a razor, but they claim that they can't find one for me." Billy sounded a bit indignant.

"There are razors to be found, but the problem is finding blades that are sharp enough. I've given up, and I'm starting to grow a beard. So what have you been doing about it?"

"Don't laugh! I've been cutting the hairs off with scissors, one by one," said Billy. "But now they're getting to be too many. Yours is really showing more than mine. But I think you're older than I am."

"I think so, too. I'm nearly twenty. And you?"

"Just turned seventeen." Billy tried to remember to keep looking at Teddy, but he couldn't avoid noticing the women in front of them who were turning to look at them.

"Steady, steady," said Teddy. "There's nothing and no one in front of us. Just keep admiring my handsome beard. Tell me, how far did you get in your home-schooling?"

"Pretty far, I think, but how can I be sure? My mothers are pretty smart and taught me all the subjects they knew best. Then they got me any books I wanted on other subjects."

"I think you might have had better home-schooling than I had," said Teddy encouragingly. "My mother died when I was thirteen. By then, I knew more than the other women in my commune. They weren't at all interested in intellectual things."

"But then ...?"

"You need to go to the Testing Lab. Katie took me there on Wednesday. They gave me some tests, and I wrote some essays. On the basis of the results, they suggested some classes and let me choose some others. This is just my second day, but I'm finding that I'm ahead in some classes and way behind in others, like calculus. Do you like math?"

"I love it! That's why I want to go the U. Where is this Testing Lab?"

"I'll take you there after lunch," said Teddy. "We're almost at the cafeteria. I'm supposed to meet Angela. I hope she's already there—she'll make a good buffer between us and the other women."

Angela saw them before Teddy saw her. She ran toward them. "That's Angela coming to meet us," Teddy told Billy, who had already stiffened. "She'll protect us."

Angela gave Teddy a quick kiss. "I see you have a new friend!" She held out her hand. "My name is Angela."

"I'm Billy."

Angela slipped between them and linked arms with them both. "I'm so glad you're going to have lunch with us," she said to Billy. "Teddy's been dying to meet some other men. Wherever did he find you?"

"I found him," Billy told her, somewhat triumphantly.

"Really?" queried Angela.

"He was lying in wait for me behind a bush at the Math Building, where he'd seen me yesterday. Like I was only a few days ago, he's nervous about being identified as a man."

"Is that right, Billy?" Angela asked. She hadn't taken her eyes off him and had held his gaze even when Teddy was speaking. Billy nodded.

"I have something to tell you both," said Angela, continuing to look at Billy as though she were speaking only to him. "There's a man in my European History class! He sits in the back and keeps a low profile, but I'm sure he's a man. I tried to speak to him today, but he ran away before I could catch him."

Billy laughed. "I hope you didn't take it personally. I've done the same thing. It's a bit scary, being out."

"If he's there on Monday," Teddy said, "maybe you could drop him a note, telling him that Billy and I would like to meet him."

"What a good idea!" Angela said, still looking only at Billy, as if to ward off any unwelcome overtures from other women. "I'll do that."

"After lunch," Teddy said, "would you have time before class to walk Billy and me to the Testing Lab?"

Angela smiled, looking at Teddy this time. "Sure thing!"

They were nearly at the steps of the cafeteria. "We'll have to go through a line to get food," Teddy warned Billy, "but just keep looking at either one of us."

Billy wasn't too happy about the idea of waiting in a line. "I've got a sandwich and an apple, so maybe I …"

Angela happily interrupted him. "Hey! So do both of us! Come on, let me lead you to my favorite tree!"

*   *   *   *

After lunch, Angela escorted her two charges to the door of the Testing Lab. "Hope to see you again soon, Billy!" she said, and waved good-bye.

Teddy led Billy into the building and up to the receptionist's desk. She immediately recognized him and was all bubbly. "Teddy! How are you? How's school?"

"Everything's great, thank you. I need to see Peggy. Is she here? Is she free?"

"Just a minute, I'll check."

There were half a dozen women sitting in the waiting room. Teddy and Billy sat down in adjacent chairs. "Keep looking at me," Teddy commanded. "Talk to me about anything—just talk."

"I like Angela. She's very pretty. I'm guessing that she's your girlfriend. Right?" Teddy nodded. "Wow, you work fast! I'd like to have a girlfriend, but, as I said, I really want to meet some more men. I hope that Angela manages to meet that guy in her history class."

His eyes started to wander around the room. "Keep talking to me," Teddy told him.

"You've got my address; I hope you'll come over sometime. I'm going to take your advice and tell my mothers how I've been spending my days. About meeting you and Angela. I never told you their names. They're …"

He was interrupted by Peggy's arrival. She quickly ushered them to her office. "Teddy, good to see you! How's it going?"

"Very well, thank you. I wanted you to meet Billy, who's in about the same situation I was in two days ago."

"That's what I guessed. So, Billy, you'd like to go to the U?"

They were soon into a conversation about the testing, and Teddy rose to leave. "I've got a class in ten minutes. Billy, you have my address and phone number. Let me know how it goes. Thanks, Peggy!"

*   *   *   *

On his bike-ride home, Teddy was deep in thought, enlarging on an idea that had preoccupied him during the last class, a biology class that he had found pretty boring and had decided not to return to.

On entering Biology House, he spotted the very woman he had been hoping to find. "Virginia! Can we talk?"

"Of course, Teddy. Any time." She drew him over to a quiet corner away from the television and the busy computers.

"I met a man today!" Teddy said. "His name's Billy, and he's seventeen. He's been sneaking out of his house after his mothers go to work. And Angela has found a man in her European History class, but wasn't able to speak to him. I don't think these men are afraid of the virus any more—certainly not if they heard Katie's talk—but it's scary being the only man out there among so many curious women."

"I can certainly understand that," Virginia said. "I wondered when it was going to get to you."

"I'm okay about it—it gets easier every hour. You just pretend that you don't see them, if they're women you don't know. But that's not what I wanted to talk to you about. I have an idea. What if we—you and I—could advertise somehow that there will be a meeting of men where we could talk about things that concern us? Whether we're safe from the virus, where to find razor blades, how to deal with all these super-curious young women, any problems we have at home ... things like that.

"I thought of maybe tacking posters onto telephone poles naming a time and place. Maybe we could use the living room here at Biology House, or an empty classroom at the U. This guy, Billy, was really desperate to find another man to talk to. And, I must admit, I was awfully glad to meet him, too." Teddy paused to catch his breath.

"Teddy, that's a great idea!" Virginia said. "Katie will be *very* much in favor it, I assure you. And I'd be happy to help you get it started. But let me tell you about men's groups in the Old Days. Some were therapy groups that were led by a therapist. Some were peer groups, and that's the kind that you're really describing. They were all men—no women allowed."

Teddy leaned forward in his chair, so excited that he could barely stay seated.

"There were only a few rules," Virginia continued. "One was that everything that was said in the room was confidential and couldn't be repeated to anyone. Another rule was that everyone must agree to respect every other person and his opinions. No name-calling. And only one person was allowed to speak at a time."

"Those are good rules," Teddy said. "They should solve some of the problems that I was worried about. So you'll do it with me?" Teddy jumped out of his chair.

"No way! It's a *men's* group we're talking about, and I'm a woman!" Virginia smiled at him. "But if it would make you more comfortable, I could be present when you start the group and explain the ground rules—and maybe the philosophy behind men's groups in the Old Days."

"That would be perfect!"

"Good. Let's talk to the others about it at dinner tonight."

*   *   *   *

Before either Teddy or Virginia could raise the subject at dinner, someone asked Dora about the hutch-building project. This reminded Solana that she needed to feed her rabbit, so she started collecting scraps of leftover salad from people's plates.

"It's all done! We did a good job, didn't we, Solana?"

"Yes! George likes it very much!"

As soon as Solana was out of earshot, Dora continued, "I have an announcement to make. That mammal that all the biologists here describe using the masculine pronoun and who seems to have been named George has dug a very deep burrow. There are some bare spots on this animal with quantities of white fur around them, so this ignorant roofer suspects that we may soon be having a population problem."

The group exploded with laughter, especially from Carolyn and the biologists. Carolyn leaned on Dora's shoulder, almost in convulsions. Dora, a smug smile on her face, patted Carolyn's head

Eva looked around the room. "Who here can sex rabbits?" Her gaze rested on her partner, Sarah, seated across from her.

"Not me," answered Sarah. "I never get it right with kittens, unless they're calicos."

"How soon do you think, Dora?" Virginia asked.

"Don't ask me, I'm a roofer!"

"We might think about raising George's litter for food," Katie said. *Cassoulet de lapin* used to be a French delicacy in the Old Days. We could have George spayed after she's done nursing this litter, or …" She stopped when she saw Solana returning to the room. "But we've got plenty of time to think about it."

Virginia quickly took control of the conversation. "Teddy has had a great idea, and we want to see what you think."

*   *   *   *

After he had put Solana to bed and read her a story, Teddy dashed next door to find Angela. She was in the living room, working at one of the computers. As soon as she saw him, she hit "Save" and "Close," and rose to greet him.

"Teddy, hi." She gave him a quick hug. "How did Billy do on the testing?"

Teddy glanced at Martha at the adjacent computer, and at Mercedes and Beth, who were sitting in armchairs, studying.

"They all know about Billy," Angela said. "I told them at dinner. And guess what? Martha got a glimpse of a man with a full beard! Maybe he's the same one Dora saw."

Teddy turned to Martha. "Really? Where was this?"

"He was leaving the History Building just as I was going in. He was wearing a hoodie, so about all I saw of him was a fairly thick beard." Martha seemed to regret that she didn't have more information for the eager Teddy.

"That's good news, Martha. I think that this fellow, whoever he is, has the right idea about beards. I'm letting mine grow too!"

Angela reached up to feel its progress. Teddy took her hand and briefly kissed it. The women in the armchairs had stopped their studying and watched the young couple with great interest and suppressed giggles.

"I don't know about Billy's testing," Teddy said to Angela. "I haven't heard from him yet." He glanced around the room, and lowered his voice. "But I have something exciting to tell you—it's about an idea I got after meeting Billy. Virginia's going to help me with it, but we can't go public with it yet."

"Then let's go upstairs," said Angela.

"Okay! Sorry, ladies," Teddy said to the other women. Angela gathered up her study materials and led Teddy up to her room.

*   *   *   *

"So tell me!" Angela said as she closed her door. "Something has you really excited."

Teddy pulled her close to him and gave her a full-body hug. "I don't think I've ever been so happy!"

He led her to the single bed that Angela—in celebration of her divorce from Cameron—had separated from its matrimonial twin and placed lengthwise against one wall. Adorned with many newly acquired pillows, it now resembled a couch.

"I'm going to start a men's group, just like they had in the Old Days. No women will be present, so we can talk about the things that pertain just to us men." They sat cross-legged on the couch, facing one another and holding hands.

Angela squeezed his hands. "That sounds great! But where are you going to find these elusive men?"

"We're going to make flyers and post them on telephone poles in the neighborhood and on campus. That should flush a lot of men out of hiding. And there will have to be advance registration. Virginia says that we should the limit the number to fifteen or sixteen."

"When will you do it?" Angela was enthusiastic. "I could pass a flyer on Monday to that guy in European, and Martha could slip one to the bearded fellow, if she sees him again."

"I don't know when we'll do it. Maybe in a few days. Katie loves the idea and definitely wants us to use the Biology House living room for the first meeting. All of the women at dinner agreed. But Katie and Virginia are both sure that the group will want to meet again, so Katie is trying to secure a room on campus that we can use in the future."

"That's good. I suspect that the women wouldn't want to give up the living room *and* access to the computers too often."

"No, and I wouldn't expect them to, either. They're pretty pleased about the idea. I have a hunch that Katie wants to alert Maureen about it."

Angela frowned. "Surely you don't think that Maureen would try to stop you from hosting this group?"

"No, I don't think that. I just think that Katie would want to give Maureen some advance notice, in view of their friendship. They've had two private conversations together recently that I know of—one Wednesday on the way home from Pendleton, and another yesterday. You saw how Katie scooted us young'uns off so that she could talk to Maureen. Something must be going on between them."

"You don't miss anything, Teddy! Have you thought of a career in psychology?"

"Only just now. Because the idea of the group is so exciting."

"You said that you'd never been so happy," Angela prompted.

"That's because I've found a way to be useful. By helping other men to come out, I can give something back to this community that has given so much to me and Solana."

"Teddy, I just love …" Angela hesitated.

Teddy raced into the pause with a mischievous "Me?" and pulled Angela closer to him.

"I was going to say that I love how thoughtful and considerate you are." Angela disengaged herself and stood up, giving Teddy a quick kiss. "I see you brought your books. I have some studying to do, too."

She went to her bed, propped her pillow against the headboard, and started in on a very thick volume. Teddy also opened a book and started reading.

A few minutes later, they glanced at each other at the exact same moment, and they both laughed. Teddy winked at her, she blew him a kiss, and they resumed studying.

Two hours later, Teddy stood up and stretched. "It's my bedtime."

"Mine, too," said Angela as she put down her book. "You'll let me know as soon as I can tell people about the group?"

"Absolutely," said Teddy. He sat down on the edge of her bed to give her a good-night hug. She held him tight, and soon he was kissing her—on her lips, on her cheeks, on her neck. Before long, they were both lying on the bed, his hands exploring her face, her shoulders, her breasts. Angela touched his face and hair, giving quick kisses to the beardless places.

Teddy lifted her T-shirt and gazed at her breasts. "You are so beautiful!" He leaned in, kissed one nipple, and sucked on the other just a little.

Angela felt her pelvis arching toward him. She sat up abruptly and pulled down her T-shirt. "Teddy, it's ..."

Teddy stood up. "Only Day Four, you were going to say?"

Angela laughed. "That's right!" She suppressed the urge to say, "Teddy, I love you, too."

Teddy gathered up his books and started for the door. Angela got up to accompany him. "I can see myself out," he said, and he blew her a kiss.

"See you soon," said Angela, who blew him a kiss back. They looked at each other and started forward for a real good-night kiss, but both of them pulled back.

"Bye," Teddy whispered. He hurried out the door and down the steps.

Saturday, August 21

Dora rang the bell and yelled, "Pancakes!" Carolyn was busy flipping them on the griddle. Dora put bottles of syrup and dishes of sliced strawberries on the long dining-room table. The crowd soon gathered.

As they entered the room, Chris explained to Teddy and Solana, "Saturday and Sunday mornings, we all get to eat breakfast together. Sometimes it's pancakes, sometimes omelets." They took plates and cutlery from the sideboard and sat down.

"We're going to a place called Little Tokyo," Solana volunteered. "Daddy's going to try to find his grandmother there." Teddy intercepted a platter of pancakes from Dora and served them out.

"That sounds exciting," Chris said. "I haven't been there for a long time. I used to love going to the Japanese garden."

"Do you know if it's still in good shape?" Katie asked. "I haven't been there for many, many years. I was a little afraid to suggest it."

"I'd give it a try," Chris encouraged. "Do you know where Japan is?" she asked Solana.

"Daddy showed me on the globe. It's a long way from here. But I think that the garden isn't so far."

Katie laughed. "It's a lot closer than Pendleton! We won't have as long a ride as we had on Wednesday."

The rest of the hosehold drifted in. They discussed their individual plans for the day and futher encouraged Katie to check out the Japanese Garden.

"Are we almost ready to go?" Katie asked.

"I need to feed George first," Solana said.

Chris was about to say, "I'll do it," but Teddy and Katie shook their heads simultaneously.

Solana left for the kitchen to get scraps for the rabbit.

"It's good for her to take responsibility for another life," said Katie, "and I'm proud that she remembered about George."

Teddy agreed. "She sees everyone pitching in, and she wants to do her share. It was so different at the commune. Big Mama dictated who had which jobs, and there was a lot of bitching about who had to do the most work."

"Okay," said Chris. "I'll hold back. But it's not just me. *Everyone* wants to spoil her."

After George was fed and watered, Katie, Teddy, and Solana set off in Katie's car. After she slid into the driver's seat, Katie asked Teddy, "Has any one volunteered to give you driving lessons?"

"Both Dora and Chris."

"Good. I hope you learn soon. I'll be happy to be a passenger more often."

"You didn't want Dora or Chris to drive today?" Teddy asked.

"It's the weekend, and I was sure they had plans. This is more of a family project, anyway. I'm a good driver, but I often get lost going to places I haven't been in a while."

They were soon traveling east on Sunset Boulevard. Katie pointed to the rows of corn in front of the walls or fences of the large estates. "See the corn? In the Old Days, people used to grow roses or other ornamental plants there."

"I noticed that you have corn out front by the street, too," Teddy said, "as well as in the vegetable garden."

"The corn out front is for anyone who needs it. Not everyone has the space or time for a vegetable garden."

"I think roses are prettier," remarked Solana.

"Is Little Tokyo on this street?" Teddy was wondering about the distance they had already traveled on one road.

"Worried that I'm getting lost?" laughed Katie. She pulled out a spiral-bound book of maps from a pocket in her door and handed it to Teddy. "Here, you can navigate. Both Takara and the Japanese Garden are on page 634. The book is a museum piece from the Old Days—it sure doesn't indicate which roads have been maintained and which to avoid. That's the top of the U on the right. I don't think you've seen this part of town before. After that is Beverly Hills. I want to take Rodeo to Wilshire, and then Wilshire all the way downtown."

Teddy studied the *Thomas Guide*, flipping pages as he investigated their probable route. Katie glanced at Teddy and marveled, *He sure caught on fast to the book's format.* Solana, in the backseat, was describing the sights to her teddy bear.

Teddy seemed puzzled. "I know we're still on Wilshire, but I'm not sure where. There haven't been any street signs for a while."

"I'm not sure either," laughed Katie. "Somewhere between Western and Vermont, I think. It's usually the individual neighborhoods that maintain the street signs, but I guess this area wasn't interested in doing that."

She stopped at the approach to a freeway overpass and looked around. "I just want to make sure that this bridge is safe," she explained. "I don't see a barricade or a sign, so I guess it's all right." She drove on. "It's so ironic. This network of freeways was built to connect all the widespread parts of LA, but, ever since the Great Disaster, it has tended to separate us. We haven't used the freeways for a long time because of the damage from the storms and the earthquake in '25. Now, they're just in the way, and sometimes the through streets get blocked with rubble."

They had reached the downtown area. Teddy gazed at the skyscrapers and remarked, "I don't see any people or scooters, or bikes or cars. Is it because it's Saturday?"

"No," Katie answered. "This area is deserted *every* day. Some of the really old buildings became unusable after the earthquake, and others were damaged by the last big storm. Those very tall buildings had elevators that used up too much electricity and windows that wouldn't open, so they were abandoned a long time ago. There's still a factory area in use, but it's farther east. Look! There's the Japanese American Community Center on the right! It looks like it's still in good shape! The garden is in the back."

Katie parked the car a few blocks away, and they walked down the block to Takara's apartment building.

"It looks well maintained," said Teddy.

"That's a good sign."

They entered the building. The lobby was clean and neat. There were a few chairs that had seen much wear. There was a row of mailboxes, which Katie and Teddy went to examine. They were much relieved to find that there was a "Takahashi" listed for 202.

Upstairs, above the doorbell at 202, there was the name Takahashi again. Below that, there was a line that had been thoroughly obliterated with ink. They rang the bell and waited.

There was no answer. Teddy looked at Katie questioningly. She punched the bell again. This time, the door was opened halfway, and a wizened Japanese lady peered out.

"Takara Takahashi?" Katie asked.

The woman was about to shut the door on them, but Katie put a foot on the door-sill and, indicating Teddy, said, "This is Machiko's son."

At the name "Machiko," the tiny woman seemed to come to life. "Machiko! Where is she?" She ran into the hallway with surprising vigor and looked in both directions. Her three visitors entered the apartment without waiting for an invitation. Takara returned, closed the door, and looked at them with unspoken questions in her eyes.

Teddy took the old woman's hands in his and said, "Grandmother Takara, I am so sorry to tell you this, but my sweet mother died six years ago." The spark left Takara's eyes as quickly as it had arrived. She abruptly sat down on the couch without offering seats to her visitors.

Teddy sat next to her and said, "She never told me about you or where she came from. I just now found out about you from Katie ... Dr. Kendall." He pointed to Katie, and then he introduced Solana. "And this is my daughter, Solana. She is Machiko's granddaughter."

"Hello, Grandmother Takara." Solana moved to a spot directly in front of her great-grandmother. Takara reached out and touched the child's head. "Tell me your name again," she said.

Solana settled herself on the couch next to Takara. "My name is Solana, and my Daddy's name is Teddy. My teddy bear's name is Bear."

Takara managed a smile for the child. When Solana cuddled up next to her, she put an arm around the child. Gradually, her story emerged. "My sister Suki and I stayed on in this apartment after our father and then our mother died. We were born too late—1995 and 1997—to marry Japanese husbands and have children.

"Suki always felt more Japanese than I did. She hated that we couldn't go to Japan to live. I didn't mind not having a Japanese husband, but I did want to have a child. Suki hated Machiko almost from the beginning—she didn't look Japanese enough. I know now that I should have taken the child and moved away from Suki. It's all my fault." Tears rolled down her cheeks.

Katie consoled her. "It's so hard to know what to do when you are put in the middle of a triangle like that. There is no 'right' thing to do."

Teddy was angry. "Suki sounds really mean to me. Where is she now?"

"She died a month ago," Takara answered matter-of-factly. "We never really got along, but I always felt that I had to take care of my little sister. But now that she's gone, the apartment feels very empty."

The group was distracted by Solana, who had gotten up to examine some paintings on the wall. Takara seemed to welcome the interruption. She joined Solana in the inspection of the paintings. "Do you like them?"

Solana was genuinely enthusiastic. "Oh, yes!"

"Which one do you like best?"

When Solana indicated her favorite, Takara took it down from the wall and gave it to her. "Then you must have it as a present. It was painted by Machiko, your grandmother."

Katie and Teddy joined them to admire the paintings.

"Machiko was an art major at the U and had sold quite a few of her paintings," Takara said proudly. She had now become more animated.

"These are wonderful," said Teddy. "I have a few of her paintings back at Katie's house. I would love to show them to you."

"I would love to see them." Takara opened a drawer and pulled out some drawings. "I have something else to show my new grandson."

"These are my mother's, too?" asked Teddy.

"No. Mine," said Takara shyly. "These are designs that I drew for the clothing factory."

"So *this* is where Machiko got her talent!" Katie exclaimed. "Do you still design for them?"

"No, I retired when I turned sixty-five a few months ago. There have been so many changes. And now, I find that I have a grandson and his very pretty daughter. I think I am ready now to hear what happened to my Machiko." The four of them settled back into their seats.

Teddy told her a little about life on the commune and Machiko's illness, without revealing the extent of their deprivations.

Takara wept silently as Teddy spoke. Then, she continued her own story: "Machiko so wanted a child that I didn't discourage her. I went to be evaluated with her. But when Suki found out that Machiko had been inseminated, she became furious and said that 'that bastard child' couldn't live here. While I was at work one day, Machiko packed up her things. She left me a note saying that she had gone to live with a girlfriend and would be in touch.

"When I had not heard from her for three days, I went to the girlfriend's apartment. Machiko wasn't there. The woman said that she had told Machiko that her apartment wasn't big enough for two more people. Machiko told her that she had seen an ad for a farming commune that was looking for new people—she would go there. This girlfriend didn't know where the commune was. I tried for years to find Machiko. I put ads in the papers, and once I went on television begging Machiko to come home so that we could find a new place to live. I don't know why, but I never thought to search in San Diego County." Takara sobbed openly.

Teddy held her as she wept on his shoulder. "We were very isolated; you wouldn't have found us. I'm so very sorry."

"But now, your family has found *you*," Katie said. Would you like to come and live with us in our commune in Brentwood?"

Takara straightened up and dried her eyes with the handkerchief that Katie handed her. She looked at Teddy and Solana, and then back at Katie. "Could I cook Japanese food?"

Katie smiled. "Only if you share it with the rest of us."

Takara hesitated. "I don't know. That might be very nice, but I've lived in this apartment all my life." She looked around the small but pleasantly furnished living room. Two large windows overlooked a backyard that contained an orange tree and several small plots of vegetables.

"I have an idea," said Katie. "Why don't we take you home with us for a week's visit? You could decide if you wanted to stay with us or whether you would rather we bring you back here. There are a lot of young people living in the house, and it can get a bit chaotic at times, so I would understand if you decided that it was more peaceful back here."

"Thank you. I would like to give it a try. I should take a few things."

"Of course! Let us help you pack," said Katie, moving instinctively in the direction of the bedrooms.

Instead, Takara headed for the kitchen and started opening cupboards. Sensing Katie's surprise, she said, "You said I could cook ..."

"Yes, of course, but we have pots at home."

"But probably not a wok. How many people to cook for?"

"Most days, we have ten for dinner. Once in a while, three houses come together—forty to fifty people—and then we barbecue."

"I'll bring the big wok and the medium wok then." Takara piled them into Teddy's arms and added some special sauces and spices from the refrigerator and the cupboard. She rummaged through a drawer and found a quantity of chopsticks—some beautifully lacquered, some stainless steel, and some disposable ones in dusty packages—to add to the heap.

"I'll take these out to the car and come back for the rest," said Teddy. Katie slipped him the keys to the trunk. Teddy noted happily that Solana hadn't asked to go with him. Instead, she was staying close by Takara's side, her eyes glued to the old woman's face. As he left the apartment, he turned to see the three heading for Takara's bedroom. Solana was holding her great-grandmother's hand.

He returned to find a suitcase packed and ready to go. It looked like a match for Machiko's bags—the frayed stickers were from hotels in Paris and Tokyo.

Katie guessed his question, and said, "The suitcases belonged to Takara's parents, who had traveled several times to Japan and Europe. Suki went with them on their last trip to Japan."

"I didn't want to go," Takara interjected. "I didn't want to miss school."

"Daddy, we're going to the garden! Grandmother Takara knows all about it."

They locked up the apartment and headed toward the car. Teddy carried the suitcase, and Solana struggled to carry the framed painting, resisting all offers of help. She did allow Takara to carry Bear, however.

In the garden, Takara led Solana around, telling her the names of the flowers and trees, and recounting the history of how the garden was created. Teddy and Katie fell back behind them.

"Katie, your heart is bigger than your house!" said Teddy. "Where do you plan to have Takara sleep?"

"I've been wondering that, too. For the first week, I'll give her my bed, and I'll ..."

"No way, Katie," Teddy said. "She gets my bed. Look at how Solana has bonded with her! A couch in the living room was good enough for Barbie, and it will be fine for me."

"That's a wonderful solution, Teddy," said Katie, a little relieved. "I hadn't thought of that. But we've got to think of something for the longer term. I'll not have you sleeping on a couch permanently."

"Maybe Angela will offer me the extra bed in her room!" Teddy said mischievously.

"Oh, no, Teddy—that would upset Solana."

"Yes, it would. I was joking! Angela's not about to offer, and I wouldn't do anything to make Solana feel insecure. I don't know for sure, but I think that she's jealous of Angela."

"I think so, too," Katie said. "We need to find ways for Solana and Angela to be alone together. Now—back to the living arrangements. There's going to be a room opening up soon in Third House. Maybe either Eva and Sarah or Dora and Carolyn might volunteer to take it."

"Not Dora!"

"You're especially fond of her, aren't you?"

"Yes! She was so wonderful at Pendleton when we couldn't find Solana and I was so scared. Solana loves her—says she's another aunt, like Chris. Which reminds me, Katie ... I've actually wondered ..."

"So have I."

"Can you look Dora up in the registry?"

"That's against the rules—invasion of privacy, and all that."

"Why hasn't she gone to the registry like Chris did?"

"Beats me!"

"Then I'll get her to go," Teddy declared.

They were joined by Takara and Solana. "We've seen it all," said a joyous Solana. "We can go home now. I want to show Grandmother Takara our garden, and she wants to meet George."

*   *   *   *

Takara sat up front with Katie. She was fascinated with everything she saw. "I haven't been out this far in years," she admitted. "After my father died, my mother sold our car. That was very disappointing to me, as I was nearly old enough to drive. Do you live near the beach?"

"No, we're up in the hills," answered Katie. "Would you like to go to the beach? Maybe we could go tomorrow, and have a picnic."

"A picnic on the beach?" shouted a voice from the backseat "Yes, yes!"

"Solana, Grandmother Takara is our guest," Teddy admonished. "We need to see what *she* wants to do."

"That's something else I haven't done for years," said Takara. "Yes, thank you, I think that a picnic on the beach would be lovely." Takara turned in her seat and looked at Solana fondly.

"Oh, goody," said Solana. "Can Chris and Dora come too?"

"We'll ask them at dinner," said Katie. "But maybe Grandmother Takara would rather have a smaller group—just family."

"But Chris and Dora are my aunts," Solana protested.

Katie and Teddy exchanged glances via the rear-view mirror. "We'll see, honey," said Teddy.

Katie changed the subject. "That's the U to our left. We're nearly home. You've been on campus, yes?"

"Not since Machiko was a student," Takara answered.

"Were you ever a student there?" Katie asked Takara.

"No, I only became college age after the Great Disaster, and things were pretty chaotic at the U at the time. The art department had pretty much collapsed."

"I remember," said Katie. "A whole group of women art professors had been on a museum trip to New York and Europe when the Disaster happened. And, of course, the men who had taught there were all dead."

After a pause, she asked Takara, "There were no other subjects you wanted to take?"

"I would have been interested in biology or botany, but I got drafted to cook at a communal dining hall. When the clothing factory started up again, I submitted some sketches, and then I designed for them for thirty years."

"We're here!" said Teddy. He was the first out of the car.

Chris ran out to greet them. "Teddy, did you find your grandmother?"

"We not only found her, we brought her home to visit and—if we don't scare her off—to stay."

Teddy helped Takara out of the car. "Grandmother Takara, this is my sister Chris."

"She's my aunt," said Solana, showing off her new knowledge of biological relationships.

Chris put an arm around Takara. "I'm so glad they found you! I'm one of the noisy ones, so I'll try to be good, so that you'll decide to stay."

"She's going to cook Japanese food!" Solana bubbled.

"You had a phone call from a young man named Billy," Chris said to Teddy.

"Hooray!" Teddy got Takara's things from the trunk and carried them into the house. He deposited the cooking materials on the dining-room table, and then he rushed up to his old room with Takara's suitcase. Then he came back downstairs to the phone.

When his call was answered, he asked, "May I speak to Billy, please?"

*   *   *   *

Meanwhile, Katie, Chris, and Solana were showing Takara around the first floor and the garden, and introducing her to the other residents as they appeared.

Solana was eager for Takara to meet George, who rather reluctantly emerged from her burrow.

"George looks pregnant," was Takara's immediate comment to the adults present.

Katie and Chris looked at each other and giggled.

"You *are* a biologist!" Katie said. "We credentialed types failed to make that diagnosis. It took Dora to point it out to us! How did you know?"

"Oh, we raised rabbits for a while. In our section of that garden behind the apartment."

Katie put an arm around her. "Takara, I do hope you decide to stay with us. We badly need a rabbit expert!"

They went upstairs to show Takara her room and help her unpack.

*   *   *   *

Teddy found Dora and Carolyn in the kitchen, preparing dinner. "Have you met my grandmother yet?" he asked them.

"No, we're too busy here," Dora said.

"I'm sorry I'm late; give me a job."

Dora handed him a big slotted spoon. "Here, stir this pot."

Teddy took the spoon and began stirring. "Mm, it smells wonderful! I wonder, will there be enough for one more at dinner? I'd like Angela to meet my grandmother."

"Of course," said Carolyn.

"Go phone her—that's faster than going next door," Dora said. The two women looked at one another and grinned.

"Okay, will do. Be right back," said Teddy as he went to the phone. *Just like Angela said, there's a very efficient grapevine in this compound,* he thought.

*　　　*　　　*　　　*

Katie, Chris, and Takara came downstairs. Takara went immediately to her kitchen supplies. Chris carried the woks, and Takara picked up the sauces and spices.

"Takara, this is Dora and Carolyn," Chris said. "They're our cooks tonight."

Takara put her load down on an empty counter-space and shook hands with them. She smiled at Dora and said, "You must be Solana's other aunt."

Dora was surprised at this, but let it pass and said, "Let's find a place for your woks. Maybe the smaller one could stay on the stove, and we could store this big one down here." She opened a deep cabinet. "It's *really* big, isn't it?"

"Katie said that you have forty or fifty people here sometimes," Takara said.

"But we barbecue outside then; we don't cook in the kitchen."

"Cooking Japanese for a large crowd is easy. I'll show you!"

"I'm ready to learn," said Dora. "I love to cook."

"Me too!"

At this moment, Angela came in through the kitchen door. She was delighted to see Teddy stirring a pot. When he saw her, he handed the spoon over to Carolyn, put an arm around Angela, and led her over to Takara.

"Grandmother Takara, this is my friend Angela. She lives next door."

Takara took Angela's hand. "I'm very happy to meet you, my dear." Teddy's eager welcome of Angela had not escaped her notice.

"Teddy," called Dora. "Can you put out the bread and butter? We're about ready to serve."

*　　　*　　　*　　　*

Dinner was a happy, noisy affair, with many people having news to report. Solana went first. "We're going to the beach tomorrow for a picnic! Who wants to go?"

Most people thought it was a great idea, so a discussion followed about what time to leave and what food should they take. Katie kept watching Takara, hoping that she wouldn't feel overwhelmed by all the people and the general tumult.

Teddy's news was next. "I just had a phone call from Billy!"

"What were the results of his testing?" Angela asked.

"He aced all the math, and will go into advanced calculus. Maybe he can help me get up to speed there! He was pretty weak in literature; Peggy recommended that he do a joint university and high school program next year and take literature and American History in high school, if the timing works out."

"High school!" Eva exclaimed.

"Yes, isn't that interesting! Peggy seemed to think that it would be all right for boys to come out and go to high school in September. She wrote a note for him to take to his mothers."

"Does he know what the note said?" asked Eva.

"I asked him the same question. He doesn't, but its contents must have been reassuring, as he said that neither mother was at all disturbed when he told them how long he'd been sneaking out."

"Something must be about to happen!" said Chris. She, Teddy, and Angela all looked at Katie for confirmation, and then at Virginia.

"Let's hope so," was all that Katie would say.

*   *   *   *

After dinner, Solana proudly showed the group the painting that Takara had given her. "My grandmother Machiko painted this!" The painting was of a little Japanese girl dressed in a kimono. There was a cherry tree in the background.

"That's me when I was about your age, Solana," Takara told her shyly. "Machiko painted it from an old photograph she found."

Everyone crowded around to admire the painting. "Where was the cherry tree?" Katie asked. "In the Japanese Garden?"

"No, Machiko added it from pictures she had seen."

Teddy opened up his portfolio of his mother's paintings. Takara was enthralled.

"This was one of my favorites," she said of the first painting, a representation of a sunrise in a meadow with a brook in the foreground and white-capped mountains in the background.

The second painting was of a field covered with wildflowers. "I think this was the same place. We took a bus trip to see the wildflowers when she was sixteen or seventeen," Takara said.

Another painting was all tan, grey, and black—some weather-worn, wooden buildings, a guard tower, and dust blowing everywhere. "This is her impression of what Manzanar must have been like," said Takara. "My grandparents were interned there. Machiko never knew them, of course."

"I always thought it was Pendleton!" said Teddy.

"Take away the guard tower, and it *is* Pendleton," was Dora's verdict. "But she painted this when she was still with you, Takara?"

"Yes, that's right. Now, *this* one, I have never seen." Takara was examining a painting of a young boy sitting cross-legged near a dirt road, his back against a tree and a book in his lap. The child is looking up expectantly, as if someone is calling his name.

"Teddy, that's you, isn't it?" Angela recognized him immediately from the charcoal drawing she had seen that first day.

"Where was this tree?" asked Dora. "I don't remember any that looked like this at Pendleton."

"No, none like this one. It must have been some tree she remembered from LA."

"Teddy," said Chris, "I hope that you'll let us frame some of these and hang them in the living room."

*   *   *   *

When it was Solana's bedtime, she told Teddy, "Grandmother Takara is ready for bed, too, and she is going to read to me." She kissed her father good-night and waved to the others.

"Good night, everybody," said Takara with an especially fond look toward Katie. Solana and Takara held hands as they went upstairs.

"I need to say good night, too," said Angela. "Thank you, Dora and Carolyn. Dinner was *so* mag!"

Teddy followed Angela to the kitchen door. "It was a wonderful evening," Angela said. "I just love Takara, and I hope she decides to stay." She reached up to kiss him. "Good night, Teddy."

"Let me walk you home."

Angela laughed. "I think I know the way! I've got final exams to study for."

"Are you coming to the beach with us tomorrow, then?"

"Sorry, Teddy. I have to put in some major book-time." Seeing his disappointment, she added, "But come over and study with me tomorrow night. I mean, *really* study."

"I'll be there, and we'll study. I'm taking exams in all my classes, too."

"Really? You don't have to."

"I want to. It'll help me know what I need to work on."
A big hug and a quick kiss, and Angela was gone.

Tuesday, August 24,
6 PM

Maureen stopped by Biology House. The door was ajar, so she went in without knocking. Many people had gathered in the living room, waiting for dinner to be served. Katie greeted her with a kiss on the cheek.

Maureen was excited. "Katie, I've come to tell you that we have final approval!"

"Really? It's a done deal?"

"You bet! I'm to go on television tomorrow night to announce that boys eight and older will be welcome in schools this fall." Maureen noticed that she already had an audience, so she started addressing her remarks to the whole room. "And that the Genetics Committee believes that it's now safe for these boys and men to leave their homes."

"About time!" Virginia shouted happily.

"Then I'll be dishing out some facts and figures about the amended Y chromosome." Maureen turned to Katie. "Unless *you'd* be willing to do that part. I wish you would."

"No, I think it would be better coming from you. But, Maureen, it should be boys *six* and up."

"Katie, life is a compromise. Accept that you've won!"

"All right, but there are going to be a lot of pissed off six- and seven-year-old boys out there," Katie said huffily. She then remembered her manners and became more appreciative. "Thanks, Maureen. I know you worked hard for this."

"You paved the way!" Maureen turned to Teddy and asked, "Would you be will-ing to come on the program and say something encouraging about being out in the world?"

Teddy looked at Virginia, they clapped their hands, and gave one another a high five. "Only if you let us make a pitch for the men's group we'd like to start," said Teddy, "for boys fifteen and older."

"A men's group? What a great idea!" Maureen was feigning surprise; she'd already had word about it from Katie. "Virginia, would you like to come on the program, too, and explain about the group?"

"Maybe," Virginia said thoughtfully, "but just for a minute or two. Most of the time should go to Teddy."

"Dinner's ready," Takara called out.

"Maureen, you must stay for dinner," Teddy declared. "This is my grandmother, Takara. This is her night to cook, and she's going to teach us how to eat with chop-sticks."

"What a treat!" Maureen extended her hand to Takara. "I'm so glad that you've come to Biology House—thank you, I'd love to stay for dinner."

*   *   *   *

After dinner, Teddy and Virginia huddled together, writing a script for the fol-lowing night. Chris settled down to watch television with Solana and Takara.

Maureen led Katie to a quiet corner and whispered, "Want to hear the latest about Pendleton?"

"Does a cat like to lick its fur?" They both glanced at the family tabby, intent on her hourly wash.

"Lauren said that it took an hour or so, but the women agreed on a structure for a cooperative management of the farm. They have a six-month trial period. The women were impressed with how much money Big Mama had been making and furious about how little of it they had seen. Everyone, of course, wanted to move into the good house with the nice bathrooms, but there weren't quite enough bedrooms, so they agreed on a rotation schedule for that."

"Sounds as though it went very well." Katie let out a sigh of satisfaction and relaxed into her armchair.

"The main disagreement was over whether Lupe should be allowed to participate. Lupe then decided that she didn't want any part of them, and so Lauren and Hazel took her back to the city and dropped her off at their hostel."

"Hm," said Katie, frowning. "I wonder how long she'll stay there. I hope they will keep an eye on her. And Big Mama?"

"Going to trial next month. On three charges, just as you predicted. That is, if her health permits. They took her to a doctor—not only does she have diabetes, but she seems to be getting delusional."

"I'm glad we intervened in time," Katie said.

*   *   *   *

After he had tucked Solana into bed and read the nightly story, Teddy went next door in search of Angela. She wasn't downstairs in the living room, where they'd had their study-dates the previous two evenings. He went upstairs, and her door was open. She was sitting on her bed with the headboard for a back rest, reading.

Teddy rushed in and closed the door behind him. "Angela, such wonderful news! Maureen is going to be on TV tomorrow night to announce that it's now safe for men and boys to come out into the world. They'll be expecting boys eight and older to go to regular school!" Teddy was so excited that the words tumbled out on top of one another.

"That's fabulous!" Angela clapped her hands. "Katie must be so pleased."

"Yes and no. She's also angry that the six- and seven-year-old boys aren't included." Teddy sat down at the foot of the bed. He started massaging one of Angela's bare feet.

Angela laughed. "Good for Katie! She was never one to settle for half a loaf."

"Nor for a loaf with a single slice missing!" Teddy said. "But the best part is that Maureen has asked me to be on the program and talk about how I feel about being out in the world. She'll also let me announce that men's group that Virginia and I have been planning—we'll hold the meeting on Thursday night at Biology House!"

"Teddy, that's just perfect!" Angela moved down the bed to embrace Teddy. His arms quickly enfolded her, and they rolled on the bed together in what had become their customary poststudy sex play. Tonight, however, his kisses were more fevered, and Angela's responses were more passionate. She purred with pleasure as he stroked her all over. Little moans emerged as his fingers found her clitoris.

But when she felt his hardened penis against her thigh, Angela sat up abruptly. "We're at the No-No place, Teddy," she said.

"Why is it a 'No-No?' I want to make love to you—to make you happy."

She gently touched the raised spot in his trousers. "I told you, back on Day One."

"And I heard you. First PhD, then baby."

"Teddy, I loved what you were doing just now, but I'm afraid that I might want to go further. And then...."

"Angela ... maybe you don't know that I know how a woman makes love to another woman."

Angela was embarrassed. "No, I didn't know, but ..."

"Who taught me? Those women I had to share my bed with, who didn't want to become pregnant." Teddy gave her an impish grin. "And they said that I was a very good pupil."

"You continue to amaze me!"

"Let me show you." Teddy slowly undressed her, marveling at the beauty of each new disclosure, then stroking and kissing every new spot. His fingers teased Angela and her growing excitement, stroking the inside of her thighs, then rising to her belly, then leaving her body altogether.

Lying beside her, Teddy kissed her with open lips, and she responded passionately. Soon, she took his hand and guided it to the spot with which his fingers had been flirting. She arched her pelvis to direct those exploring fingers. She moaned, then cried out, "Oh, Teddy! Teddy!"

Teddy stood up and gazed down at the relaxed and grateful Angela. He kissed her lightly. "Gotta go. Watch me on TV tomorrow?"

Angela sat up. "You're leaving?"

Teddy smiled. "Exams tomorrow, you know!"

There was a bench under the avocado tree in the Biology House garden. Teddy stopped there and, with a glance at the upstairs windows to make sure that he wasn't being observed, slid down his trousers and achieved his own climax.

Wednesday, August 25, 7:30 PM

The living room of the Santa Monica apartment wasn't large. It contained little more than a good-sized couch, two armchairs, a coffee table, and a television set.

Twenty-year-old Don sat in the middle of the couch, his customary place when he watched TV with his mothers.

"Edith, Dottie, come on," he shouted. "The program is about to start." And indeed, the young anchorwoman was announcing, "Welcome to this special program. Dr. Maureen Gabriel, the head of the Genetics Committee, has a very special announcement to make. Dr. Gabriel …"

Edith and Dottie hurried in from the kitchen and seated themselves on either side of their strapping son.

Maureen appeared on the screen. "Thank you, Barbie," she said.

"I didn't know she was white," said Edith.

"She must be a lot older than she looks," added Dottie.

"Hush," Don said. "This must be important. They've been mentioning it every hour, reminding people to watch."

His mothers obediently stopped their comments.

"I have a most exciting announcement to make," Maureen began. "But first, I want to give you some background. A few of you have been aware that our boys seem to be living longer. There are rumors of boys eight and ten, and even teenagers living amongst us, sight unseen except by their caretakers. People have been wondering what's happening. Has the virus died out?"

Don was getting excited. He sat on the very edge of the couch. He broke his own decree of silence and said to his mothers, "See? I told you so!"

"Well, we don't know if the virus has died out or not." Maureen paused and looked around, perhaps at a studio audience.

"She doesn't know about the virus," Edith said. "It's still not safe."

Dottie looked at Edith behind Don's back. She put her finger to her lips.

"What we *do* know," Maureen continued, "is that our male children are not dying at ages one, two, and three, as was happening as recently as ten years ago. Instead, they are surviving at the same rate as male children in the Old Days. Actually, the survival rate is slightly higher, probably because they haven't experienced rough play on a playground or risked being hit by a veggie truck."

"So it's true," murmured Dottie. She linked an arm with Don.

"We believe that this survival rate can be attributed to a research program headed by Dr. Katie Kendall. She experimented with altering the Y chromosome to make male children immune to the Gender-Specific Virus—the GSV. About twenty years ago, 5 percent of our inseminations were with this experimental amended Y-chromosome sperm. The results compared to the control group were so good that, fifteen years ago, we started using this experimental sperm for *half* of the inseminations."

"That's me! I was in the first group!" Don exulted, jumping off the couch and dancing around.

"For the last ten years, we have used *only* the experimental sperm," said Maureen. "And, as I said before, these boys are living even longer than boys did before the GSV. So now, the announcement. We believe that it is safe for all men and older boys to come out of hiding. Beginning with the next school term, which starts a week from now, schools will be open to all boys aged eight years and older. For men seventeen and older, there is a Testing Department at the U. If you are interested in going to the U, we encourage you to come and be tested, to find out both what you have learned and not learned compared to women your age and, more importantly, what you would like to study or what kind of work you would like to train for."

Barbie interrupted. "This is really exciting news, Maureen. But let me get my arithmetic straight. You say that all boys who were born during the last ten years have this experimental Y chromosome, and therefore are safe. But what about the boys and men whose mothers were inseminated before that, and might not have this safe Y chromosome?"

"Yes, what about that?" Edith demanded of the face on her TV screen.

"I'm afraid that all the boys who did not have the experimental Y chromosome have died. So, you men and you boys over ten, you and your mothers were very lucky! It's safe for you to come out of hiding and join our society. And we hope you will do so."

"See? I told you so!" Don repeated.

"These numbers and addresses on the screen are for the Testing Lab and the Registry. We hope that you will also go to your Neighborhood Centers, where people can advise you about schools and jobs."

Don, perched next to Dottie on the arm of the couch, busily wrote down all the information.

"As you may have heard," Maureen continued, "some young men have already been venturing out. I want you to meet ..."

"Excuse me, Maureen, but I have another arithmetic question. If all boys under ten have this good chromosome and are safe, why can't boys of six and seven go to school too—and the younger ones to kindergarten and preschool?"

"Barbie, that is *such* a good question!" Maureen looked for all the world like a cat who had just purloined a piece of fish from the dining-room table. "There was a lot of debate about the age issue. We are reasonably certain that the GSV is no longer a threat. Otherwise, we would not be making this announcement. However, we can't *guarantee* anyone's safety. We might have another earthquake, and your child's school could be destroyed. He might be hit by a truck. The mothers of the very young boys have been so responsible and so vigilant. A mother of a six-year-old boy might want another two years to keep her boy close to her. But, if you disagree, be sure to take that disagreement to your Neighborhood Center."

"Or maybe to the local school?" Barbie suggested.

"Of course!" Maureen said. "And now, I'd like to introduce a young man who has been a part of our society for a little over a week. Those of you who attended Katie Kendall's birthday lecture last Tuesday may recognize him. This is Teddy Vlatas."

A tall young man with short black hair and definite signs of a future black beard appeared on the screen. "Hello, everybody, and particularly you men and boys out there. I'm Teddy. A week ago, that was the only name I had. Now I know my whole name, Teddy Vlatas, and something of my ancestry. I'm half Greek and a quarter Japanese and a quarter Latino. You, too, can find out about your sperm-donor ancestry by going to the Registry. Can we have that number back on the screen? Thanks, Barbie.

"I was brought up in a very isolated farming commune with twelve women. I had never been out of this Greater San Diego commune until I decided to leave and come here to go to the U. So, I've had more learning to do than you fellows who have mothers who go to work and bring home news of the community. A lot of things that were big surprises to me, you fellows already know.

"But it's been a wonderful learning experience for me. I live at Katie Kendall's Biology House with Katie and seven other women, all of whom have helped me learn how this new society works. I did the testing at the U, which is really a lot of fun. It's not something that you pass or fail, so don't be scared of it.

"I've had five days of classes at the U, and spent a terrific day at the beach on Sunday. But there's been one *major* drawback. Except for Billy, a really neat guy who I met Friday on campus, I've seen *no other men!* So I am overjoyed by this announcement that Maureen has just made. Please, come out and keep me company!

"We need to find one another, we need to talk, we need to help one another with all the adjustments that being out in the world requires. So I had this idea of having a meeting of just men—fifteen years and older. We're doing it tomorrow night. That's my phone number and e-mail address up on the screen. The first fourteen men to call …"

"That's it! I'm going!" Don ran to the telephone.

"Don, wait! We need to talk about this!" Edith started to run after him, but she was caught by Dottie, who embraced her. "Edith, sweetheart, we have to let him go."

"But is it safe?"

"You heard what Maureen said. Boys with this new Y chromosome are surviving at the same rate as in the Old Days."

"But maybe he doesn't have this new Y-thing."

"He must. Otherwise, he wouldn't still be here."

"I thought that it was because we never let him get close to another boy, and fed him all the right foods, and …"

"All of that helped, I think. But don't you see what this means? Donny can have a real life … go to the U … get married … have children! Edie, we can be grandmothers some day!"

Don raced back into the room, exultant. "I have a place in the group!" He hugged Edith first. "It's going to be all right, Edith. I promise you that I'll be safe."

As he hugged Dottie, she murmured, "I'm so happy for you."

Don kissed her, and then turned his attention back to the screen. Barbie was asking a question. "Teddy, I'm still hung up on the numbers here. Why are you limiting the group to fellows fifteen and older?"

"There are two reasons. First of all, we're all in that first 5 percent group, so we will always be a small group compared to the number of males in the 50 percent group and the 100 percent cohort. We are the vanguard. If we can learn quickly how to be men out in the world—how to avoid making any major mistakes—we'll be able help the younger ones. We could even be a model for them.

"And secondly, what about women and sexual relations? That's got to be a bigger issue for us than for an eight-year-old!"

Don looked at Dottie and grinned.

Barbie laughed. "That's for sure! Any comment you want to make on that topic, based on your eight days in LA?"

Teddy's face flushed just a trifle. "No, not really. Not publicly anyway." After a moment's hesitation, he added, "But there is one thing I want to say. I'm on campus with hundreds of gorgeous women my age, each one prettier than the last. I'd love to meet each of them—as a friend, as a fellow student—but some of them come on so strong, are so curious to see what a man looks like, even to touch him, that I have to run away from them. I don't feel like they see me as me—as Teddy—but just as a kind of example of some new species."

"That must be an awful feeling, Teddy. I'm so sorry." Barbie extended her hand as if to touch his arm, and then quickly pulled back.

Teddy reached out for her hand. "That's all right, Barbie—you're my friend. And thanks for understanding." He drew her hand to his lips and lightly kissed it.

"He seems like a very nice young man." Edith was brightening to the idea of Don going out into the world. "Maybe he'll become a friend of yours."

"I would imagine," said Barbie, "that all this attention will make it hard for you to find a real girlfriend. I assume you do want one!"

"I've already found one," Teddy said with a happy smile. "And that's all I'm going to say on that subject," he warned Barbie.

"Before I introduce Virginia, who will describe what men's groups were like in the Old Days, I want to say hello to an old friend." Teddy leaned forward as if to bridge the distance between them. "Domenica, I hope that you are watching this program, or at least hear about it. I owe you so very, very much. I want you to know how very happy I am, and it's all thanks to you and your encouragement."

Teddy looked offscreen. "Could we have my phone number and e-mail address on the screen again? Thanks."

Teddy again looked intently into the camera. "Domenica, I hope this reaches you. I want to keep you in my life. Now here's Dr. Virginia Reynolds, professor at the U, therapist at the Counseling Center, and friend extraordinaire."

*   *   *   *

Virginia and Teddy rode home together on Virginia's scooter, Teddy with his arms around her waist, talking excitedly into her ear. "How do you think it went? Do you think we'll get enough men for the group?"

"I'm certain we will," Virginia predicted. At the same time, she was thinking, *I'm too old to be feeling this happy to have this young man's arms around me.* There was a bump in the road, and Teddy clasped her more tightly. *I hope I didn't do that on purpose.*

When they reached Biology House, they saw Maureen's car. She was waiting for them and entered the house behind them.

They were greeted with a round of applause by the full Biology House crew, most of whom were standing.

"Daddy, Daddy," Solana ran to Teddy. "I saw you on television!"

Teddy picked her up and kissed her. "So you recognized me!"

"Of course, silly Daddy." She touched the stubble on his cheek. "But this looked blacker."

"That's good." He kissed her again and put her down. Turning to the group, he asked, "Were there any phone calls?"

The group roared with laughter.

"It never stopped ringing," Chris said. "Your group was nearly full before the program ended. And now there's a waiting list large enough for a second group."

Teddy and Virginia high-fived.

"And no one has checked the e-mail yet," Dora added.

Katie moved toward Teddy. "We were all so proud of you. I want to thank you for mentioning the Registry in your first breath. That was good of you."

"First things first, Katie," said Teddy as he kissed her.

"You were wonderful, Maureen." Katie said. "I suspect that there will be some boys showing up for first grade next week. Maybe kindergarten, too."

"You think so?" Maureen was playing innocent, but had a twinkle in her eye.

"I know so, and I love you for it." Katie gave her old friend a big hug and a kiss on the cheek.

The phone rang. Chris shouted, "Your turn, Bro. I hardly got to see any of the program because of that phone."

As Teddy left to answer the phone, Katie said to Maureen, "Do you suppose that there could be a rebroadcast of your program? There was a lot of important information there."

"I'm sure there will be. Barbie told me before I left that they're airing your birthday talk this weekend."

"Barbie was cute," Katie said. "I assume you put her up to those questions."

"No, I didn't." Maureen was genuinely innocent this time. "She came up with those 'arithmetic' questions herself. I was as surprised as you, but not above grabbing the bait."

Eva spoke up. "I think we should have Barbie and Maddy to dinner soon."

Carolyn agreed. "Good idea. It's time I gave Barbie a checkup to see how that baby is coming along."

"I'd never have guessed that she was pregnant," said Sarah, "the way she looked on the tube."

Teddy returned from his phone call, more exuberant than ever. "That was Domenica! Evidently there was a buzz about our program in Greater San Diego, and they somehow hooked into the LA signal."

Katie was cynical. "That Council is so fearful that LA is going to be more prosperous than them, or do something that will impede their progress."

"I invited Domenica to dinner," Teddy said. "She thinks that she can get a merchandise delivery to LA next month—she'll let me know."

"Dora and I have two-seater scooters," Chris said. "We could go down to San Diego as a party some weekend!"

"Me too," said Virginia, looking at Teddy mischievously. "I've got a two-seater. That way, we could also take that mysterious girlfriend you mentioned, but didn't name!"

People looked around at one another, some smiling and some giggling. Solana was in neither group.

"Daddy, do you have a girlfriend?" she asked.

"Yes, honey, I do. Or at least, I hope so."

"Oh." Solana went to cuddle next to Takara. She started to put her thumb in her mouth and then stopped herself.

"Solana, it's way past your bedtime," Teddy said. "Let's go upstairs, and we'll talk about this." Teddy held out his hand. Solana took it almost reluctantly, and they climbed the stairs, Teddy waving a silent "good night" to those in the living room.

"Well, I really put my foot in it," said Virginia. "You'd think I would know better."

"It's good that you said it," said Katie. "You brought it out into the open. Solana had been too quiet—not like her usual rambunctious self—ever since Barbie used the G word."

"She's jealous of Angela, of course," said Chris. "But I have an idea. If her two aunts—Dora and me—could be conspicuously friendly to Angela, seeing her as one of the family, insisting that she come to dinner, and so on, Solana might get more comfortable with the idea of Angela in her life."

"Good idea," said Dora. "I'll go along with that. But I'm *not* Solana's aunt."

"How do you know?" Chris asked. "Have you been to the Registry?"

Katie, delighted, cautioned herself to be quiet and not join in.

"No," Dora admitted.

"Why not?"

"I don't know. I guess I'm scared to find out. Because I'm not smart like you and Teddy."

Katie could keep quiet no longer. "Not smart? Holy mackerel! Who knew George was pregnant? Who is always the first person around here to come up with clever ways to fix things?"

"Thank you, Katie," said Carolyn. "I keep telling her that 'smart' is a lot more than book-learning and advanced degrees."

"And it's not just Solana who thinks you're her aunt," said Katie. "Teddy and I both think you *must* have Peter Vlatas genes."

"If you're truly scared to go to the Registry, let me go with you," Chris offered. "I see you as a sister anyway, but it would be so *mag* to have you be my biological sister as well."

Dora, fairly overwhelmed by all the attention, agreed.

Teddy came downstairs and rejoined the group.

"That was a fast story," remarked Eva.

"We had a little talk," Teddy said, "and I think that she's feeling reassured. But she wants Grandmother Takara to read to her."

Takara got up from the sofa. "I will be happy to do that. It's my bedtime, too. It's been a lovely and exciting day." She kissed Teddy good night. "I am very proud of you, grandson."

"I think I'll run over to see that 'mysterious girlfriend' of mine," Teddy said, "and see if she is still speaking to me after Barbie's question." He gave Virginia a friendly hug and left.

"Takara has had four days to try us out," Chris said to Katie. "Do you know how she's feeling? I hope she'll stay."

"She hasn't said a word to me on the subject." Katie answered. "I haven't asked, as I'm afraid that she might interpret it as a suggestion that she leave."

"Has she figured out yet where Teddy sleeps, and that she has his bed?" Dora asked. "Knowing that might make her decide to go back to her apartment. Personally, I think that she likes it here despite all the confusion. She certainly is attached to Solana."

"Eva and I have been thinking the same thing," Sarah said. "And we have a solution. We've heard that a couple is moving out of Third House. Katie, could we have ..."

"Excuse me, I had the floor," Dora said. "Nobody wants you two to move out. I've been thinking, and I have a long-term solution and a short-term solution."

"Let's hear it!" said Chris.

"We could build a room and bath next to your building, against that mostly blank wall. The bathroom would be next to your bathroom, to minimize plumbing costs; the bedroom would essentially go on that hillside that isn't being used for anything."

"I like that idea, Dora," said Katie, "but it sounds pretty long-term."

"Yeah, what's the short-term?" asked Chris, who rather enjoyed her separate existence out in the back.

"The maid's room over there," said Dora, pointing past the kitchen, "the one that's used as a junk room. You can barely walk through it to get to the bathroom. If people would clear their junk out, I could get the shower working again ..."

"What a great idea!" said Chris. "Teddy could slip out to go to History House without anyone noticing."

The group tittered at this image.

"Dora, that is a genius idea," said Virginia.

"I'm all for it. It's been criminal not to use that space," said Katie. "And down the road, when I get old and don't want to climb stairs any more, I could take it over."

Eva and Sarah exchanged glances. "Well, of course, we like the idea too, as we really didn't want to move away from Biology House," Eva said.

"How about this, then," Dora proposed. "You all have two days to get your stuff out of the room. Anything still there on Saturday morning will be taken to the Neighborhood Center for giveaway. I'll fix the plumbing, and the rest of you can paint the room. Teddy can move in Sunday night."

Chris took over. "Discussion?" Much shaking of heads. "Let's vote, then. All in favor?" All hands were raised.

*   *   *   *

Teddy arrived at History House to find the entire household waiting to congratulate him. One by one, they offered a "Good show," or "You were terrific," or "Well done, Teddy," and quickly scurried up the stairs.

"Wow, my speech about the college women really scared them off! Now I have *them* running away from *me!*" He led Angela to the couch.

"Nonsense! It's late, they have exams tomorrow, and they just wanted to give us some time alone." She hugged Teddy, and he kissed her. "I thought you were great. But tell me how it was for you."

"I loved doing it," said Teddy. "It was easy. But I did get thrown by Barbie's question about girlfriends. How did you feel about my answer?"

"I loved it! It's not going to take people very long to figure out who this girlfriend is. I'm very happy that it's me."

They kissed a bit, and then Teddy pulled back. "There's been one complication," he said. "Solana isn't happy that I have a girlfriend. I think that this is a holdover from Pendleton, where I was forced to have those other women in my bed, and she felt excluded. Also, they weren't loving or motherly to her at all."

Angela was distressed. "Oh, dear, what can I do?"

"We could spend some time together—the three of us—with the two of us paying more attention to her than to each other. Go somewhere on our bikes. Saturday, maybe."

"That would be fun! Let's do it—we'll take a picnic lunch."

"And maybe you could come and read a bedtime story to her. She thinks that you don't really like her—despite the picture books, despite the wardrobe from Roweena—because you've never offered to read to her."

"I'd *love* to! I never thought to ask—I thought I'd be intruding, really. After all, she has you, Katie, Chris, Dora, and now Takara." Angela paused. "But tell me, have you had any phone calls for your group?"

Teddy laughed. "That's exactly what I asked when we got home tonight, and they laughed and laughed. Evidently, the phone rang constantly. There are enough sign-ups for two groups."

"Outstanding, Teddy!" Her fervent embrace and his kiss in response led to some more smooching.

Angela pulled back to ask, "Will you do a second group?"

Virginia and I haven't had time to talk about it, but I suspect so. We have Room 232 in Roberts—my lucky room ..." Teddy paused to kiss her. "... if the guys tomorrow night want to meet again. Virginia assures me they'll want to do just that. So that same room might be okay for a second night with a second group."

"This is *so* mag!" She suddenly turned sober. "The phone rang a lot here, too. Mostly other history students who were happy for me, telling me what a lucky woman I am. But one call was from Cameron. She was so nasty that I hung up on her."

"Baby, I'm so sorry." Teddy held her tightly. "Are you afraid of her?"

"No, not really. Martha says that I should watch my back, though."

"We'll bike to the U together. And I'll meet you at the History Building instead of the cafeteria. What time should we leave tomorrow?"

"My first exam is at nine. Should we leave at eight?"

"That's good for me." They both stood up. Teddy held her tightly, then kissed her on the forehead. "Don't stay up too late studying." And he left.

Thursday Evening, August 26

The door to Biology House was ajar, but Don rang the doorbell anyway. Chris stopped arranging chairs to answer it.

"You're here for the men's group? Come on in. My name's Chris. I live here."

"My name's Don."

"I took your call last night!" Chris lit up in recognition. "I remember that you were pretty excited."

"I still am—I can hardly wait for the group to start!"

"Well, it'll be another half-hour. Come help me with the chairs. We need a circle of sixteen."

"I'm sorry I'm early. I didn't know how long it would take to get here, and I didn't want to be late."

"No problem. I'm happy to have some help with the chairs. There are some more in the dining room." Chris pointed them out. "So, did you bike or walk or …?"

"I walked. I'm twenty years old, and I don't know how to ride a bike! My mother Dottie has promised to teach me this weekend."

"That's cool. You get to see a lot more and go a lot farther on a bike. I suspect that there's a lot you want to see, if this is your first day out."

"You know it! I walked all over my neighborhood today."

"What do you think you want to do now that you have all this new freedom?" Chris was genuinely interested. "What kinds of books do you like to read?"

"Geography! History! Travel! That's pretty silly, isn't it, when you can't leave Greater Los Angeles?"

"I don't know about that. There are lots of changes coming. For instance, there will probably be a caravan going to Atlanta in a year or so."

"Really? Are you going?"

"I've thought about it, but this trip is mostly for scientists. I can, however, fix computers, and I know a bit about car repair."

"Hey, maybe I should learn car repair!"

"Why not? But get your driver's license first!"

Eva popped into the room. "Chris, I just need fifteen minutes at the computer. Oh, I didn't realize anyone had come for the group."

"Eva, this is Don." The two shook hands.

"I'll split before the group gets started," Eva promised as she settled herself in front of the computer farthest away from the circle of chairs.

"Eva is a biology student at the U," Chris explained to Don. "And you have a final tomorrow, right, Eva?"

"That's right," said Eva. Her screen was aglow, and she was obviously uninterested in Don.

"Are you at the U as well?" Don asked Chris. "What are you studying?"

Chris was flattered to be seen as someone of college age, but then she realized that he hadn't been out in the world long enough to be a good judge of age.

"I finished at the U eight years ago," she answered with a laugh. "Part science and part lit major, if that makes any sense. But I'd been repairing and building computers since I was a teenager, and that's what I do now."

"Wow! I love computers. I'm a lot better at the software than my mothers, but *building* one ..."

The circle of chairs was completed, and Chris and Don sat on adjacent chairs to continue chatting.

Solana bounced into the room. She immediately placed herself before Don and held out her hand. "Hello, I'm Solana. What's your name?"

"It's Don." He solemnly shook the child's hand.

"This is my niece," Chris said.

"How old are you?" Don was entranced with this playful little girl.

"I'm four, and I'm starting school next week, but I won't be in the same class as my friend Roweena." Solana's words tumbled out of her mouth.

"Well, that's both good and bad, I guess." Don gave Solana his full attention. "What's that you have in your hand?"

"Food for my rabbit. Do you want to come meet George?" Solana was fascinated by this person, only the second man she had ever seen.

"Solana," said Chris, "weren't you asked to stay out of the living room tonight, like the rest of us?"

"Yes, but ..."

"This isn't the way to George's hutch. Go feed her, go up to your room, and I'll come to read you a story in a little while."

Teddy came into the living room. "Solana!" he said sternly, "What are you doing here?" Then he saw Don and greeted him with a different voice. "Oh, hello, first arrival! I'm Teddy."

"Yes, I know you from the TV. I'm Don." Don offered his hand.

Chris gave Solana a look that said, "Now!" and Solana scooted away, but not without a wave to Don, who returned it with a smile.

"Very glad you could make it," Teddy said. "I'm so excited to be doing this."

"Me too," said Don.

Chris made a quick exit up the stairs. "Good group, guys!" she said, too quickly for Don to react.

The doorbell rang, and Billy dashed in.

"Billy, my man!" Teddy shouted. They gave each other a brief hug that consisted of slapping one another on the back.

Don was a bit disconcerted as he watched this demonstration of male friendship.

"Don, this is Billy—the man that I met on campus Friday."

Billy held out his hand for a handshake. Don was relieved not to be expected to hug him. *But I could have handled it*, he reassured himself.

Eva left her computer and the room unnoticed by all except Billy, who waved at her.

"Thanks for the nice mention you gave me on TV, Teddy. I went to the campus today. The women were being different; they pretended not to notice me until I noticed them and smiled, and then they would smile back. And this is the best part ..."

The doorbell rang, but since the door was open, Teddy waited to hear the rest of Billy's story.

"There was a really pretty girl sitting at a table by herself, so I took my tray over and asked, 'May I join you?' And she said, 'Sure thing.' Her name is Terry, and she had already guessed that I was Billy."

"That's out of sight," said Teddy.

"You're one fast worker," said Don with admiration.

The doorbell rang again—a longer and more insistent ring. Teddy went to the door. There stood a woman rather imperiously holding the hand of a small boy who, thought Teddy, couldn't be more than fifteen, if that.

"I'm Velma Lansdowne," the woman announced, "and this is my son, Pablo, who signed up for your group without my permission." She entered the room with Pablo, who didn't say a word.

"We're so very glad you came, Pablo," said Teddy. "Thank you for bringing him, Ms. Lansdowne. The group should be over at 9:30, if you wanted to come back for him then." Teddy went to the door to hold it open for her.

"No, I intend to stay," the woman said.

"I'm sorry, but that won't be possible. You see, this is a men's group—*just* for men." Teddy spoke in his most conciliatory tone, while at the same time wishing that he could legally throttle the woman.

"I would be happy to run him home in my scooter when the group is over," added Virginia, who had entered the room in time to hear the complete exchange.

"But *she's* here," argued the overprotective mother.

"This is Dr. Virginia Reynolds. She is going to talk about the ground rules for groups, for a maximum of five minutes. And then she's going to leave." Teddy and Virginia both said, "Good night, Ms. Lansdowne," as they ushered her to the door and closed it after her.

Pablo suddenly found his voice. "Gee, Teddy, you really handled her!" His appreciation was obvious.

The doorbell rang with another lengthy blast.

"This had better not be your mother, Pablo," said Teddy grimly as he went to the door. Instead, a burly man with a fully grown beard burst into the room. He was wearing a sleeveless T-shirt that revealed a well-developed chest and heavily muscled arms. He had a heavy leather satchel slung over one shoulder, and he dropped it to the floor. *He looks older than twenty,* Teddy thought. *But he can't be. Must be the beard.* He unconsciously touched the stubble on his own cheek.

"I'm José. You're Teddy. I liked what you said last night." José shook Teddy's hand vigorously and then moved into the group, introducing himself to Billy and Don.

When he came to Pablo, he said, "You're just a little squirt! Are you old enough to be here?"

Pablo looked him square in the eye, even though he had to raise his head to do it. "I'm Pablo. I'm fifteen, and I like your beard." He extended his hand.

José shook it gently. "Pablo, you're okay!"

The rest of the group arrived all at once. Teddy was no longer able to meet and greet each new arrival at the door. The men introduced themselves to one another. Teddy stood back and watched, noticing which ones quickly felt at ease and which were initially hesitant to shake hands.

"I think we're all here," Teddy announced. "So can we all take seats and get started?"

Once they were all seated, Teddy introduced Virginia. "You probably remember Virginia from last night's TV. I've asked her to meet with us for a few minutes to run through those rules for groups again."

"Rules and suggestions," said Virginia with no preamble. "The first rule: Everything that is said in the group is strictly confidential. It's not to be repeated to anyone—family, girlfriend, anyone at all. If anyone feels that he can't handle this restriction, we'd like him to leave now."

Everyone nodded except Pablo, who spoke up. "If you're worried about me, Virginia, don't be. I don't tell Velma *anything*."

"Good for you!" said Teddy.

Virginia continued after a warm smile to Pablo. "The second rule is to respect one another. Respect one another's opinions. It's fine to disagree, but do it respectfully. No name-calling." Several of the men waved their hands above their heads in agreement.

"The third rule is that only one person is to talk at a time. I have a suggestion about how you can manage this. There used to be a Native American custom of the 'talking stick.' When they held their powwows, only the person holding the stick was allowed to speak. If someone in the group had a question or a comment, he could raise his hand. If the speaker wanted to recognize that person, he would point the stick at that person. When he raised the 'talking stick' vertically, the person's time was up. I would suggest that tonight, you start with introductions, and go through them with a minimum of interruptions. And now I pass this fireplace poker on to Teddy and take my leave. Have a good group!"

"Thank you, Virginia," said Teddy as he accepted the 'talking stick.' Several in the group waved their hands above their heads as Virginia left the room for the kitchen area.

"My name is Teddy Vlatas, as you know. I'm nearly twenty. I live here at Biology House with my four-year-old daughter, Solana. I have just started at the university. I don't know yet what my major will be, but that doesn't seem to make any difference. People want you to experiment and find what you really want to do and are also best suited to do. I was brought up in a farming commune in San Diego, but that's a long story for another time, so I will pass the talking stick to ..." He held it up and looked around the room.

Don raised his hand and took the poker. "My name is Don, I've just turned twenty, and I'm so excited to be here. I don't know about the rest of you, but I've never seen another man before tonight, except in old movies. I have two mothers who love me very much and love one another very much. They're really good to me, but lately I've been so restless—dying to get out of the apartment, to go somewhere by myself, to meet new people. One of them, Edith, was really scared about me coming here tonight. Neither of them wanted to let me come here by myself; they thought I would get lost." Don snickered. "Well, we have an old *Thomas Guide* of Los Angeles streets that I have studied, so I knew exactly how to get here. I collect maps. I think I want to go to the U, but now I mainly want to explore the world outside of our apartment. But I've said enough. Who's next?"

Billy was the first to hold up his hand, so Don passed him the talking stick. "I'm Billy. I'm seventeen, and I can hardly wait until I have a beard like you, José. The cabin fever got to me several weeks ago, and I started sneaking out of the house after my mothers left for work. I mostly went to the campus, which is close to our house. At first, I thought that I wanted to meet girls and have a girlfriend, but then I got scared off. They were so aggressive—like Teddy said on TV—that I started hiding. Then I started trying to meet another man—and boy, was I glad when I found Teddy."

Billy gave a "thumbs-up" to Teddy and continued. "He took me to the testing lab, and I'm down for some courses at the U and some others at high school. And today, I met a real pretty girl named Terry, who's eighteen. But that's enough about me, who wants …

"Oh, one final thing! What was so ironic was that when my mothers found out what I had done, they were tremendously pleased! They had decided that it was safe and wanted me to go to the university, but had hesitated to suggest it for fear that I would think that they were pushing me out of the nest. Isn't that a hoot? We three are a whole lot closer now. They had been bugging the Genetics Committee for some time to make the announcement that it's safe for men and boys to come out of hiding. One of my mothers—the biological one—is a hotshot in the math department, and I think she had a lot of influence in the decision. Along with Katie Kendall, of course. Now, who's next?"

Several men had their hands raised. José looked as though he might take the talking stick whether it was offered to him or not, so Billy chose him.

"I'm José. I'm twenty, and I know I look older. I got my beard when I was really young." He smiled at Billy. "I envy you guys who were raised by loving, committed couples. I bet you didn't know that the fucking Genetics Committee would also inseminate a woman in a commune after evaluating the commune for harmony and stability and whatever else. Well, my commune might have been all of that twenty-one years ago, but when I was about ten, it started to fall apart. There was constant bickering, and a lot of people left. The woman who I think was my biological mother died. Anyway, no one felt any responsibility toward me any more. I started exploring when I was about twelve, and I split for good when I was eighteen. I had sense enough to know it was safe outside, even if the fucking Genetics Committee didn't. Do you guys realize that they must have known *ten years ago* that it was safe? That little boys weren't dying any more? The fucking Council has robbed us of ten years of our lives!"

Sensing the group's restlessness, José tried to lighten up a little. "So I found an empty apartment and raided garbage cans and gardens for food. Then, one day, I was watching a construction crew doing major repairs on a house. The forewoman spotted me and asked me if I wanted a job. So I said 'why not?' and she put me to work. First they had me doing easy stuff—mostly fetching and carrying heavy things. But gradually, I learned how to do most of the jobs at the site, and now I'm pretty good at all of them! The women were great—they shared food with me and never asked questions. Then ..." José stopped abruptly. "But I've gone on long enough. Squirt, you want to be next?"

Pablo took the proffered poker. "I'm Pablo, and I've got a story to tell, too, and I'm eager to tell it. But first, I want to hear the rest of *your* story, big guy." He pointed the poker squarely at José.

"Yeah!" and "Don't lead us on like that and drop us," were shouted at José.

José looked around at the group. "Okay, thanks. The truth is, I'm in deep trouble and don't know what to do about it. I hadn't been working construction long before I got involved with one of the women, Cookie. I moved into her place, and everything was great until she got pregnant. We were both excited about the baby. We'd worked it out with the forewoman about a pregnancy leave for Cookie in the last months, and easier work before that. After the baby came, we were going to take turns staying home with it, and Cookie's mother was going to be there two days a week. Then, last week, Cookie went for a prenatal checkup—at my urging, damn it!—and this fascist quack notified the fucking Registry!" José's anger was mounting again. "So Cookie went in and gave them her ancestry back to Eve. They squeezed her so hard that she demanded that I go in. I wouldn't go—I don't know who either of my parents was. So she kicked me out."

José seemed about to cry one minute and reverted to anger in the next. "I can't go back to my job because the Registry is looking for me and Cookie told them where we work. So I'm back to the empty apartment and garbage cans. But now I have to keep hiding. That's it." He looked back at Pablo.

Several men raised their hands. Pablo pointed the poker at Billy.

"I feel for you, man. Why don't you come home with me tonight—sleep in a bed with clean sheets, raid the refrigerator? I'm pretty sure that my mothers would be cool about it."

Pablo next pointed to Teddy. "I don't have a bed to offer, but a couch here in the living room. I sleep on one of them, and both are comfortable. There's plenty of good food in the fridge. And, if you'd be willing, I can offer you a talk with Katie Kendall in the morning. I'm sure she could help you."

Pablo pointed the stick back to José, who was very touched by the two offers. "Thank you both. Let me think about it. I've already taken a lot of time."

Pablo pointed the stick at himself. "I'm Pablo, and I'm fifteen. There's just my mother Velma and me. Some of you saw her earlier." The tone of his voice gave permission for audible groans from those who had witnessed Velma's performance. "Little does she know that I've been out of the house every day for a year, getting the lay of the land and meeting people. Hanging around the high school, mostly. I'm short, I don't have a beard yet, and I can still pass for a girl. Especially when no one is used to seeing boys.

"Some months back, I met a girl named Pamela, and we started hanging out together—nothing romantic, we just had lots of things to talk about. I finally let it slip that I was a guy and wanted to figure out a way to go to high school this fall. She already knew what a bitch Velma was. Pam told her parents, and they told her that I could come to live with them and go to high school. I was close to running away when Velma and I saw you"—Pablo smiled at Teddy—"and Maureen on TV. I went to the phone right away and was lucky to get a place in the group.

"When Velma realized what I'd done, she said, 'I can't give you permission to do that.' So I said, 'Either I go to the group or I'll run away, and you'll never see me again.' I think that scared her, so we agreed that I could come to the group as long as she escorted me here. I thought she was going to try to talk you out of taking me—too young, emotionally disturbed, subject to seizures, whatever. I never *dreamed* that she thought she could stay and listen! Anyway, the good news is that I went to the high school this morning and registered for the fall term. All they wanted to know was my name and home address. They asked me what year I thought would fit best, so I told them the junior year, since Pam is going to be a junior. That's all about me, except I hope we have time tonight to talk about sex."

With that, Pablo passed the talking stick to the next man.

*   *   *   *

When the last man had finished his introduction, Teddy stood up and was handed the talking stick. "Guys, it's 9:15. I'm expecting that doorbell to ring in exactly fifteen minutes, so there are a few things I'd like to settle before then. Several of you have used the phrase 'next time,' so I'm assuming that you'd like to continue. Right?"

Everyone agreed heartily. "Fantastic! Virginia was sure you would want to—I didn't know, never having been in a group before—so she arranged for us to have a room on campus for our exclusive use. It's Room 232 in Roberts Hall, the same day—Thursday—at the same time. Is that cool with everyone?"

They all agreed. "One more thing," Teddy suggested. "How would you feel about making up a roster with names, addresses, e-mail addresses, phone numbers—in case you want to get in touch with one another between group meetings? Only those who want to."

Everyone wanted to, so they shifted over to a computer and took turns entering their personal data. They were nearly finished when the doorbell rang.

"She's early!" Teddy groaned.

"Let her wait," said Pablo.

"Okay, everybody, check what you wrote before I print out copies for you," said Teddy.

"Don't print one for me," said Pablo. "Velma goes through my pockets. She'd *love* to know who's here."

The doorbell rang again, and this time the finger seemed glued to the bell.

Virginia came into the living room. "Do you want me to get that?"

"Would you, Virginia? But could you go out the kitchen door and intercept her at the front. She does *not* need to know who's in the group." Teddy was more than annoyed at Pablo's mother.

"I'll go with you, Virginia," said Pablo. "Good night, everybody! This has been terrific. I can't wait until next week."

"Wait a minute, little Squirt!" José went over to Pablo and stroked his soft cheek. "You're the greatest! Thank you. Hey, I feel something growing here!"

"You're not so bad yourself, Big Guy," Pablo replied, and he disappeared into the kitchen behind Virginia.

The others milled around talking, first waiting for the copies to emerge from the printer, and then waiting to make sure that Velma had gone. Virginia finally came back in and said, "They're gone—and in a veggiemobile!"

"Pretty royal delivery," said one of the men. Then most of them left in a group, still excited about the evening and chatting with one another.

Don found Virginia and asked her, "Do you know where Chris is?"

"Go out to the building behind the house; that's her computer shop," answered Virginia, somewhat puzzled.

"I just wanted to thank her for helping me feel okay about being here," Don explained, and he exited out the door to the garden.

Virginia started up the stairs to her bedroom, saying good night to the three left below.

Teddy and Billy looked at José expectantly.

"Yeah, well, I've been thinking," José began. "I really want to get back with Cookie. I want to be there when the baby comes. And if the only way I can make that happen is to go to the fucking Registry, well, that's what I have to do." He turned to Billy. "You said your house was close to the U and the Registry is on campus, right?"

"Right."

"Well, if the offer is still good, I'd like to sleep at your house tonight and then go to the Registry first thing in the morning."

"You're on, man!" Billy was tremendously pleased.

"Good decision!" said Teddy. "I like it that you want to make things right with Cookie."

José turned to Teddy. "Now, about that offer of food … I haven't had much to eat today, and I'm starving."

"Let's go get it!" and the three headed for the kitchen.

Teddy opened the fridge and pulled out an assortment of leftovers: Japanese noodles, beans, some chicken, and a pitcher of lemonade. Billy poured himself a glass of lemonade. José put a helping of everything on a plate and started wolfing it down.

When he saw José's appetite, Teddy started grilling a cheese sandwich for him. "I think that you might have a pleasant surprise tomorrow at the Registry. I doubt they'll be as bad as you think."

"Yeah? Have you read *1984?*"

"No, but I've heard about it." Teddy answered. "I don't think that book was on the Marine Corps reading list."

"What about the Marine Corps?" José saw Teddy's remark as a complete *non sequitur.*

"That commune that I mentioned was in Pendleton, on the old Marine Corps base. The only books I could read growing up were the ones that marines and their families had left behind."

"That's a bummer," José said.

"That commune was a dreadful place. I was born there, and my birth was never registered. If it had been, the Registry would have kept track of me, and I would have been rescued many years ago. I probably would have read *1984* by now."

"I think my birth was registered," José said. "I vaguely remember going to a place when I was about five where grownups asked me a lot of questions, measured how tall I was, stuff like that."

"That sounds like the Registry," Billy said. "But we all went back for examination every five years or so. I think my last time was two years ago. They need to keep track of us to see how this amended Y chromosome is doing. Also I think there are three kinds, so they want to find out which one is best. There's a motto hanging at the Registry—something like 'Our Children are Our Gift to the Future.'"

"Well, this Registry never bothered to keep track of me," José growled.

Teddy was pleased that at least it was no longer the "fucking Registry," and decided to change the subject. "What kind of scooter do you have?" he asked José. "I'm just learning about the different kinds."

"It's got a sidecar, which is either good for a passenger or hauling stuff. One of the perks of being in construction," José explained.

*   *   *   *

Don made his way across the backyard to a building that was probably once a detached double garage. The garage doors were gone, and in their place was a single door whose top half was frosted glass. Don could see that lights were on inside, but he could find no doorbell. "Chris!" he called out. "Are you there?"

"Come on in," she answered.

Don opened the door and went in. All along one wall was a row of tables loaded with computers and printers in various stages of repair. The only vehicle was Chris's two-passenger scooter with its extension for hauling computers. The other half of the building had been converted to living quarters, and was separated from the workshop by a five-foot wall.

Chris peered over the wall, surprised that the male voice belonged to someone other than her brother.

"I'm sorry," Don said, confused. "I didn't know you lived here. I thought it was just your shop."

Chris emerged into the work-space. "Don't be sorry. We're very informal around here." She was wearing pajamas and a raggedy old sweater.

"I just wanted to thank you for helping me find my way into the group. We're meeting again next week."

"You're welcome. I'm glad it went well."

"I was wondering when could I see you again."

Chris was surprised, but not displeased. "If you're free tomorrow, you can do my computer rounds with me—to see if you'd like that kind of work. Teddy has come with me once or twice, but he has classes tomorrow. Nine o'clock?"

"That would be great!" Don gave her a big hug and left. Chris was a bit startled, but receptive. *He must be used to hugging his mothers*, she thought as she climbed to her bed in the loft. There was a big smile on her face.

*   *   *   *

Back at the house, Teddy saw the other two men off. Billy was sitting in the side-car, holding José's large and very heavy satchel on his lap.

Teddy quickly cleaned up the kitchen and started out the back door. Remembering a difficulty he had experienced two nights before, he went back into the house. He went into the maid's room and was surprised to see that half of the clutter was gone. He went into the bathroom, opened a cupboard, and found a small hand towel, which he put into his book-bag.

He crossed the space between the two houses, wondering whether it was too late for a visit. There was no light in Angela's room, which could be a good sign—but could also mean that she had gone to bed and put out the light. Rather than going to the front door and ringing the doorbell, he continued through the garden to the glass doors to the living room and rapped on them lightly.

Angela immediately opened the door and let him in. She gave him a quick kiss. "I was afraid you weren't coming! How did the group go?"

"It went so *well!*" He gave Angela a big hug and led her over to the sofa. "I wish I could tell you what happened."

"But you can't; I know that." Teddy kissed her on the lips and neck, and a hand reached for a breast. She pushed him away long enough to ask, "Did the group run over?"

"No, we stopped on time. But there was one guy who …"

"Stop! You're about to tell me something that maybe you shouldn't."

"You're right! Thanks! Well, I think I can ethically say that three of us had a snack afterwards in the kitchen, and that's why I'm late." He resumed his nibbling and kissing and stroking.

A thought occurred to him, and he pulled back. "You haven't asked if we're going to meet again."

"No, because of *course* you are!

"You had more faith than I did," Teddy said, stroking her cheek.

Angela stood up. "I have something to show you up in my room."

He followed her up the stairs. Angela closed the door behind them. Teddy set down his book-bag and looked around the room. He didn't see anything unusual and turned to face Angela.

She smiled at him seductively, then slowly undid the buttons of her blouse. She quickly opened the blouse to reveal her breasts and then, as quickly, closed the blouse. When she reopened the blouse yet again, Teddy sprang to help her take it off.

She brushed his hand away. "No, no. This is a look. Don't touch." She pushed him into a chair. And then she threw away her blouse in the old burlesque-show style.

Next, she played with removing her shorts, shifting them up and down on her hips while swaying to some unheard music. She twirled around and, seeming to have forgotten about her shorts, played with removing her sandals, tossing each in turn into Teddy's lap.

Teddy was entranced and having difficulty with the "no touch" restriction, especially after the shorts came flying at him. He was standing again by the time the panties came off. He reached down to gaze upon and then touch that magical area, now fully revealed.

"Not yet," cautioned Angela. She proceeded to undress Teddy, first pulling off his T-shirt and kissing his nipples. She started to unzip his pants, but Teddy warded her off. He kicked off his sandals and then did a male version of her striptease, unzipping and rezipping his jeans, lowering and raising them and then kicking them off. His underwear revealed a full erection.

Teddy then did a little twirl, losing his shorts in the process. As he faced Angela, he threw his arms out to his sides, saying "Ta-da!"

Angela gasped quietly, then timidly came forward to touch his penis. Emboldened, she kissed it gently, and then started to stroke it—first gently, then more firmly.

"If you keep doing that, I'm going to come!" Teddy was very excited. He loved what was happening, but, at the same time, realized that his book-bag was nowhere within reach.

Angela reached under her pillow for a hand towel not unlike the one in Teddy's book-bag. "I'm not going to stop until you do." With that, Teddy eased onto her bed and gave himself over to that happy ecstatic moment. His body went limp. His long walk from Pendleton, his panic when he couldn't find Solana, his nervous anticipation about leading a group—all fell away from him as though they had been events of a long-ago past. He drifted off to sleep for a few minutes, and then realized that Angela was snuggled up against him on her bed.

"My angel," he murmured. Then as he awakened more fully, he asked, "How did you …?

Angela giggled. "I guess you didn't know that I knew how men and women made love in the Old Days. Too bad you couldn't have stayed longer on Tuesday; I could have shown you then!"

"You wonderful, foxy woman, you!" Teddy gave her a long, exploring kiss on the mouth, and his fingers went straight to her expectant clitoris. The little moans of pleasure came quickly, and Angela gave herself over to successive summits of ecstasy as Teddy experimented with different ways to help her achieve them.

Finally spent, Angela rolled over onto her side. Teddy cupped his body around hers and pulled the covers over them both. She reached for his hand and held it against her breast, and they fell asleep.

*   *   *   *

Angela woke up with a start and looked at the clock. "Teddy! It's 3 AM!"

"Mm," was his sleepy answer.

"I think you want to be at home and asleep on that couch when Solana wakes up."

"Oh my God, yes!" Teddy sat up, searched for his scattered clothes, and hurriedly put them on.

Angela sat up in bed to watch him, making no move to cover her breasts.

Teddy lightly kissed each nipple and then her lips. "This has been the most wonderful evening of my life."

"I think we'll have many more," she answered, kissing him back. Then, on a practical note, she asked, "We're on for Saturday—you and Solana and I, right?"

"Of course. What time?"

"Early. Right after breakfast. Funny thing—Dora came by earlier tonight and asked me if I had any plans for Saturday, so I told her that the three of us were going biking. She thought that that was a great idea and suggested that we take her scooter and stay out for the whole day. Biology House must be up to something. Do you know what?"

"I haven't a clue. I hope you accepted the offer of the scooter."

"Of course! I also asked her if it was okay to give you a scooter-driving lesson, and she thought it was a fab idea."

"Wait a minute! Is her scooter one of those double-seater ones, or does it have a sidecar?"

"Sidecar, so when we start out, I can drive and you sit in the sidecar with Solana on your lap. The picnic supplies will be in the front basket or strapped onto the rear."

"Good. That should be safer for Solana than the two of us trying to sit on that second seat. Are we biking to school tomorrow?"

"No. I've had my last exam, and I intend to spend the whole day on my dissertation. Go, Teddy." Angela raised her head for a good-night kiss, and Teddy tiptoed away down the steps.

Saturday,
December 16, 2062

The backyard of Biology House was festooned with streamers and balloons. There were two long tables with two punchbowls each, cups, and flowers. The tables were surrounded by people helping themselves and chatting. Katie and Maureen, seated together on a covered patio up on the hillside, watched the people milling about the yard and caught snatches of their conversations.

"You've made so many changes over the past two years, Katie. I hardly recognize the place. Where are the chickens and rabbits?"

"We moved them to the far edges of the History House and Third House lots and took down all the boundary hedges. We now have all this great open space." Katie extended her arms to indicate the expanse. "We're expecting quite a crowd today."

"I'm so happy that I was able to get home in time for the commitment ceremony."

"I want to hear about your two consultancies. Were you pleased?" Katie looked fondly at her long-time friend.

"Yes and no. First of all, I was pleased that both communities thought so highly of what we've achieved here in LA that they would invite me. I was discouraged and somewhat dismayed to discover that it was the very individuals who invited me to come and consult who were the problem personalities in both places!"

"So what did you do?"

"I met with all the neighborhood committees and heard their complaints, went on TV, and gave out my e-mail address. The men haven't been as successfully integrated into those communities as they were here. One reason was that those Councils took even longer than ours to put out the word that it was safe to come out into the world. The men there are pretty resentful about it. Both places will be having Council elections in March."

"Pretty much the same formula that we used two years ago?" Katie asked.

"Exactly the same," said Maureen, smiling.

"Is Lauren running in San Diego?"

"Yes, but I don't think she has a chance. The Council's lack of oversight of Big Mama's place is just one of the many issues that the Liberty Party is using against her."

Katie clapped her hands in glee.

"But tell me about your two couples." Maureen was ready to change the subject.

"Well, Teddy hasn't decided on a major. He's taken a lot of computer, engineering, and biology courses, but doesn't seem to be close to a decision. He's still drinking in knowledge about *everything*. He's still doing men's groups two nights a week. Angela continues to be very focused on her studies and her writing. And on Teddy, of course. And now ..."

They were interrupted by Solana. "Hello, Grandmother Maureen. You've been gone a long time. I missed you." She hugged Maureen.

"I missed you, too! How have you been?"

"I'm in school now! I can read and write. And I'm going to have a baby brother. His name is Peter." Solana at six was definitely more mature, but she hadn't lost her exuberance.

"I see Roweena. I've got to go. Bye!" And the child was gone.

Katie anticipated Maureen's next question. "No, they don't know the sex of the baby. We'll have to wait another three months to find out. Solana is determined that it will be a boy. And yes, if it's a boy, they will name him Peter."

"That must make you very happy, Katie." Maureen patted Katie's arm.

Katie smiled and nodded.

"And if it is a girl?"

Katie's pleasure was obvious as she answered, "They wanted her to be named Katie, but I've insisted not. So they've settled on Lisa."

"I noticed the two signs." Maureen pointed to the two signs further up the slope. They were shaped like headstones in the cemeteries of the Old Days. One read, "Lisa Kendall, 1922–2014;" the other, "Carmen Perez, 1967–2045."

"That's such a nice touch," Maureen continued. "When did that happen?"

"On my last birthday. It was a surprise from the commune."

"You have such great young people here, Katie. But you didn't finish talking about Angela."

"I was just going to say that she has about another year until she finishes her dissertation, and then I expect that she will be the Twentieth-Century American History expert on the faculty."

"Wonderful! But won't the baby interfere with her timetable?"

"I don't think so. Chris and Dora canvassed all of us except Teddy and Angela. Everyone said that they would love to have a commune baby. They told this to Teddy and Angela, and, two months later, Angela was pregnant! Peter or Lisa is going to be raised cooperatively, and her mother will finish her degree on schedule."

"That's lovely! But where does everyone sleep? You seemed to be running out of room when I left town."

Katie laughed. "We've been playing musical beds. First, Teddy moved off the sofa into the maid's room after we cleared out all the junk. Then Dora designed and—with the help of José, a man from Teddy's first group, and his girlfriend—built that bedroom and bath." Katie pointed toward an addition to Chris's quarters.

"It had first been intended as a future room for Teddy and Angela. However, the kids felt that they should be in the same building as Solana, so Dora and Carolyn took the new building, and Teddy and Angela moved into their room—which, after mine, is quite the largest bedroom in the house."

"They're still together, then, Dora and Carolyn?" Maureen asked.

"Very much so. I don't know what's happening in San Francisco and San Diego, but I've noticed something interesting here since the men surfaced. Most of our same-sex couples have become even more sincerely committed to one another than before. Dora and Carolyn, Eva and Sarah, and Barbie and Maddy, who moved into Third House with their youngster." It's almost as if they're proclaiming that they would have coupled even if there had been men available back then when they first met.

"All this is keeping you young, Katie. You look great."

"Thank you. I'm doing fine. There was one other move: Takara had a fall and twisted her ankle. Teddy had just moved out of the maid's room, so she moved into it, to avoid the stairs. Solana was quite delighted to have a room of her own."

"How is Takara?"

"She's getting a bit frail. She's in her room resting now. Solana will get her before the ceremony starts."

"And what about Chris and her young man?"

Katie spotted a group of women approaching a spot just below them. "Sh!" she said to Maureen. "Let's eavesdrop."

Several solicitous friends were accompanying Edith and Dottie. Dottie was saying to one of them, "We like Chris a lot; we think that she'll be good for him."

"It's fine with me that he has a partner," Edith added. "I like Chris. No, really I do!" This last was directed at another friend, who evidently was feeling dubious about Edith's proclamation. "But I'm scared about this trip to Atlanta. I think they're crazy to do it."

"When do they leave?" the first friend asked.

"Next week," Edith said. "I'm afraid that they'll never come back."

Dottie put her arm around Edith. "Don learned car repair especially so that he would be selected for the trip. It's always been his dream to see the world." The group drifted out of earshot.

Maureen asked, "That was …?"

"Don's two mothers," Katie replied. "I don't know their friends. Edith, the second mother who spoke, had a total conniption fit when Don moved into Chris's place."

Katie laughed, remembering that time. "We had no idea that there was a romance blossoming under our noses! We just thought that Chris was teaching Don computer repair and offering him a place to stay to get some relief from Edith's constant anxiety about his safety. Don was one of those men who hadn't dared to venture out until you gave your 'all clear' signal, Maureen."

"How did they meet? And what's this about the trip to Atlanta?"

"Don was in Teddy's first men's group. And as for Atlanta, those middle-aged geneticists who are going need a support group—someone who can keep the computers running and someone who can repair cars and trucks—that would be Chris and Don. Don learned car repair from Jo and Marie—they're very unhappy that he'll be leaving, if only temporarily."

The two couples had emerged and were standing in a line greeting the new arrivals.

"I should go pay my respects," said Maureen, somewhat reluctantly.

"No, let them find you. You had a long sail home from San Francisco. Stay here and watch with me."

"All right," said Maureen gratefully. "It *was* a rough sail, and I'm tired."

"Look who's just arrived! Recognize them?" Katie nodded in the direction of two women with two toddlers in tow.

"Is it? Yes, it is!" Maureen exclaimed. "Alicia and Isabella!"

They watched as Teddy and Angela embraced the newcomers and leaned down—Angela with some difficulty—to speak to the children. Solana and Roweena appeared almost instantly and took charge of the toddlers.

"Did you know that they've become a committed couple?" Katie asked, still keeping her eyes on the group.

"No, I've been out of the loop."

"Well, as they told Teddy and Angela, they'd been through so much together at Pendleton, and their kids got along so well from the beginning, that they decided to make a life together. They both got counseling at the U. One result for Isabella was that she became reconciled with the mothers she had run away from. Then, when one of the mothers got very ill, the young women moved to San Diego to help out the other mother. So we haven't seen anything of them for nearly a year now."

"That's such a happy ending! Those two women were lucky to get pregnant and get a passage out of Pendleton," said Maureen.

"And their kids are lucky to have Peter for a grandfather," Katie reminded her.

"Squirt!" The word had been roared out somewhere below them. Both women looked down to see a very large man greeting a young boy by lifting him off the ground and swinging him around.

"What on earth is going on?" exclaimed Maureen. "Someone should rescue that little kid."

Katie laughed. "That little kid is Pablo, a first-year student at the U. The big guy is José, who helped Dora build that new building. They were both in Teddy's first group. When Pablo ran away from his overbearing mother, he headed straight for José's and Cookie's apartment. I think he lived with them for several months; he lives on campus now."

"I'm surprised that *you* didn't take him in, Katie," Maureen teased.

"No way! Biology House was the first place that dreadful woman came looking. Speaking of taking people in, are you ready to give up living alone? There will always be a place for you in the compound. In fact, I've been keeping Angela's old room in History House empty, just in case."

"Katie, you're such a dear to keep offering! Let me think about it. These last two years have taken a lot out of me, so maybe …"

Virginia was waving to them from below.

"I see that Takara is out on the porch," said Katie, "so I think that Virginia is trying to tell me that it's time." Katie got up to leave the cozy hillside perch. When Maureen rose to join her, Katie said, "Stay here if you like. It will be standing room only down below, and you do look weary. There's a sound system, so you won't miss anything."

Maureen watched as Katie carefully descended the dozen steps while holding on to the railing. Once on the ground, she and her cane forged into the crowd, stopping to greet a few people as she made her way onto the large porch that extended half the width of the house.

There was a crowd of people on the porch. Some were seated, like Takara and Angela, but most were standing. Maureen could identify the people from Biology

House, but there were a number of unfamiliar faces. Teddy adjusted the microphone for Katie.

The crowd gathered closer to the porch. *Why aren't they starting?* Maureen wondered as she noticed a whispered consultation among Teddy, Dora, and Katie. Dora had started to go down the few steps to the yard when Roweena, Solana, and two boys their age appeared from around the corner of the house. Solana dashed onto the porch and perched on the arm of Angela's chair.

Katie then spoke. "Hello, everybody. I'm Katie Kendall. Welcome to Biology House! Some of you have come a very long way, and we are very honored that you did so. This is a very special day for me, for several reasons. First, I am so happy to have my dear friend, Maureen Gabriel, back in LA after two years away doing missionary work. There she is, up on the hillside."

Maureen was taken totally by surprise as two hundred people turned to look at her. Some clapped, some waved. She happily waved back.

"And what a special treat it is to be a witness at the commitment ceremonies of these people whom I love so dearly. They are, to me, the children I never had—Teddy, Chris, Angela, and now Don." She looked at each one fondly, her eyes misting just a little.

Katie stepped back as Chris and Don came forward. Each of them kissed her, and Don escorted her to a prominently placed armchair. Chris then went to the microphone and waited for Don to join her. With arms around each other's waists, they intoned, in unison, "Hello, everybody! Thank you for coming and being our witnesses."

Chris separated from Don, took the mike, and said, "I'm Chris Vlatas, and I want to introduce my mothers, Hannah and Ruth, and thank them for being here and for the very happy home they gave me as a child." The two mothers stood and shyly acknowledged the applause. "They had despaired of my ever finding a partner, but thanks to Maureen"—Chris gave a wave toward the hillside—"I finally met the perfect partner for me. Then there's my sister, Dora, and her partner, Carolyn." Both stood and waved to the audience. "My niece, Solana." A very energetic wave from Solana. "Katie, my brother Teddy and his bride and my friend Angela, and everyone at Biology House. Thank you all for being our witnesses on this very special day." She turned to Don.

"I'm Don Knox-Turner, and I want to introduce my mothers, Edith and Dottie." He then spoke to them directly. "It must have been disappointing for you when I turned out to be a boy, considering all the hazard and extra care that involved, but I never sensed any disappointment from you, and have always felt very cherished." They stood, waved, and were applauded.

"There are some very special men from my men's group here—Billy, José, Pablo … I'm going to miss you guys! And, of course, Katie, Teddy, Angela, Solana, and everyone at Biology House. Thank you so much for being here today."

Don turned to Chris. He took both her hands in his and gazed into her face. "Chris, I love you. All those years, when I was cooped up in the apartment trying to imagine what life could be like outside, I never dreamed it could be you, the life that we've had, the life that we are going to have, or this wonderful adventure that is beginning soon.

"I pledge to you to be an open, honest, loving partner, in sickness and in health, on smooth paved roads and on bumpy ones, to share the covers equally, and—when can I see you again?"

Chris burst into laughter at their private joke, hugged him, and hung onto him for a minute while she convulsed with laughter. Then she pulled back, looked at him and took both of his hands in hers.

"I love you too, you crazy, wonderful man. I love your sense of adventure. I thank you for awakening mine. This trip is going to be the greatest. I pledge to you to be an equal partner, to not hold back, to be open and honest, to continue to demand my share of the covers, and, in answer to the question, 'When can I see you again?'—just wait until I get you home tonight!"

The audience burst out laughing and clapped loudly. José whistled loudly. Chris and Don threw their arms around one another and kissed.

They separated, looked at one another, and went to the mike. In unison, they said, "And now, Teddy and Angela." With that, they stepped to the back of the group.

Teddy held out a hand to help Angela out of her chair. Angela's arm was around Teddy's waist, and his arm went around her shoulders. Together, they said, "Hello, everybody. Thank you for coming to be our witnesses."

"I'm Angela Kendall, and, in addition to Chris and Don and everyone at Biology House, I have some special people to thank for coming here to be witnesses. First, my mother Cindy." Cindy stood briefly and waved to the applauding audience. "You taught me what it takes to be a genuinely loving mother, and I hope I can do as well for Solana and …" She patted her protruding abdomen.

"Peter!" Solana supplied the missing name. Angela laughed along with everyone else.

"There's my childhood sister, Evvie. My buddies from History House—Martha, Mercedes, and Beth. And special thanks to Katie"—Angela blew her a kiss and Katie waved back—and to Solana." Solana jumped out of her chair, ran to hug Angela, and remained by her side.

Teddy took over. "I'm Teddy Vlatas. I'm so touched to have all of you here. Thank you. I'd like to introduce a very special lady—my grandmother, Takara Takahashi. Teddy left the mike and went to embrace Takara, who remained seated. The audience clapped and she waved back. Teddy returned to the mike and picked up Solana and kissed her. "Thank you, Solana, for being part of the ceremony and being the wonderful daughter that you are."

He carried her over to where Dora was standing near the front of the porch, and put her down. Dora immediately put her arms around the child, holding her in front of her.

Teddy returned to the mike. "I want to thank my two sisters, Dora and Chris, and everyone at Biology House. I love you all. You fellows from the group—Don, Billy, José, Pablo. And a very special lady who came up from San Diego. If it weren't for that very good road map that you drew for me, I wouldn't be here today—Domenica Ortiz."

There was much applause from the audience.

Teddy continued, "And Katie, dearest Katie. I owe you so much. Your being here and your approval means everything to me." Katie blew him a kiss and the audience again applauded.

Teddy took both of Angela's hands. "Angela, I fell in love with you on Day One in Room 232. And every day since then, I have learned more about you and have fallen more deeply in love. It's now Day Eight Hundred and Fifty-Two, and we're just beginning." Angela tried to suppress a giggle, but failed.

"I love your loyalty, your caring for me and Solana, your dedication to your dissertation, your sense of humor, and your down-to-earth sensibility. I pledge myself to be an open, honest, loyal, and supportive partner, to do my share of the diaper changing, and not to bitch too much about 'when are you coming to bed?'"

There was laughter from the audience.

Angela took his face in her hands and kissed him. "Teddy, I love you more every day. You have taught me so much about love. I love your sensitivity, the way you behave with every new person you meet. I love that you are so brilliant. I love that we can talk about anything and everything together. You are such a good father to Solana; Peter or Lisa is going to be very lucky to have you for a father.

"I promise to be an open, honest, loyal, and supportive partner to you and a loving mother to Solana, and to Peter, or Lisa, and whoever might follow. And," she added seductively, "please keep reminding me that it's bedtime if I ever seem to forget."

There was laughter from the audience and another wolf-whistle from José. Teddy kissed Angela tenderly. They both turned back to the mike.

"One final thing …" said Teddy.

"… we want to publicly thank everyone at Biology House …" Angela continued.

"… for saying the magic words that helped us to decide …" this from Teddy.

"… to have this Biology House baby." Angela concluded their joint statement, patting her rather large belly.

Laughter and applause from the audience.

Together, Angela and Teddy said, "And now, to History House for refreshments. See you there!"

Epilogue

2072

There is much bustle in the backyard of Biology House as the TV crews position themselves to film the memorial for Katie Kendall. First, they take a shot of the signs on the front of the house—"Biology House" and the newer "Vlatas House." Then, they photograph the tableau at the top of the hill, where two more hand-painted signs have been added to the original two: Takara Takahashi, 1995–2065 and Katie Kendall, 1980–2072.

Angela and Teddy are both on the faculty at the university. She teaches in the history department; he has a research appointment to study the interface between biology and computers. They have three children. Solana paints and writes poetry, but this radiant teenager thinks that she would like to be a clothing designer. Or a psychologist. Or an actress. But definitely a mother.

Their nine-year-old boy is indeed named Peter. Their toddler is named Lisa.

Virginia has been reelected to the board of the Council.

The 2062 outreach trip to Atlanta was successful. There were no major mishaps, and the scientists were well received. Chris and Don have not returned to Los Angeles to live permanently. On the way to Atlanta, they encountered several smaller communities that needed their particular skills, so they have spent their time going back and forth between them. They have encouraged many young people to volunteer to move to these places, and vibrant societies are being built there. On their last trip to LA, Edith and Dottie persuaded them to leave their young daughter with the older women to raise, arguing that children needed a secure home. Chris and Don agreed, partly because, unbeknownst to Edith and Dottie, they are probably going to be shipmates on the first voyage to Europe.

The game of musical chairs at Biology House has continued. After Takara died, Katie moved downstairs into the maid's room, but not before Dora and José had enlarged it and given it an exit to the garden and its own patio. Teddy and Angela then moved into the master bedroom. Maureen moved into History House in early 2063.

Dora has trained enough young men to be roofers so that she seldom climbs a ladder any more. Instead, she is much in demand as an architect. She enlarged the building that she shares with Carolyn to include a room where Carolyn does primary care for the immediate neighborhood two days a week. The other days, she is a senior surgeon at a nearby hospital.

Katie remained vigorous until the last few weeks, when her mind began to wander. She started addressing Teddy as "Peter." At dinner on her last night, she announced, "It's time for me to go home. I'm going home now." The group thought she meant to her room, and Teddy escorted her there. Only Maureen was not surprised when it was discovered the next day that she had died in her sleep.

About Janette Rainwater

Jan Rainwater is retired as a clinical psychologist. She was in private practice for many years—PhD from UC Berkeley, 1964—and has led over five hundred workshops on five continents. The most recent ones were in Russia and Eastern Europe, where she trained psychotherapists in gestalt therapy and psychosynthesis. Her 1979 self-help book, *You're in Charge: A Guide to Becoming Your Own Therapist*, has been translated into eleven languages.

She describes herself as "a lifelong anti-fascist and pro-humanist." She did graduate work in American History at The Johns Hopkins University under C. Vann Woodward, worked in the presidential campaigns of Henry Wallace, Adlai Stevenson, and the Democratic opponents of Ronald Reagan and George Bush, was a Peace Corps psychologist in Colombia, and has visited Nicaragua, other Central American countries, and Cuba with different delegations including Witness for Peace and Food First.

She has been a board member of numerous political organizations and was a researcher for Barbara Trent's documentary film *Cover-Up: Behind the Iran-Contra Affair*. She also is a friend, mother, grandmother, gardener, and householder.

In an earlier phase of life as a faculty wife and Cub Scout den mother, she did photojournalism and wrote children's books. She is now widowed and lives in Pacific Palisades with her wonderful dog, TomPaine.

978-0-595-42379-8
0-595-42379-5

Printed in the United States
84739LV00002B/1-48/A